D0898274

SPECIAL MESSAGE TO READERS

This book is published under the auspices of

THE ULVERSCROFT FOUNDATION

(registered charity No. 264873 UK)

Established in 1972 to provide funds for research, diagnosis and treatment of eye diseases. Examples of contributions made are: —

A Children's Assessment Unit at Moorfield's Hospital, London.

•

Twin operating theatres at the Western Ophthalmic Hospital, London.

•

A Chair of Ophthalmology at the Royal Australian College of Ophthalmologists.

•

The Ulverscroft Children's Eye Unit at the Great Ormond Street Hospital For Sick Children, London.

You can help further the work of the Foundation by making a donation or leaving a legacy. Every contribution, no matter how small, is received with gratitude. Please write for details to:

THE ULVERSCROFT FOUNDATION,
The Green, Bradgate Road, Anstey,
Leicester LE7 7FU, England.
Telephone: (0116) 236 4325

In Australia write to:

THE ULVERSCROFT FOUNDATION,
c/o The Royal Australian College of Ophthalmologists,
27, Commonwealth Street, Sydney,
N.S.W. 2010.

TRAVIS QUINN, OUTLAW

When he left on the stage to Socorro he was Dave Callahan, a respected cattleman. Moments later he was Travis Quinn, the notorious outlaw, with men lining up to take a shot at him. He rode a deliberate trail into outlaw country where he figured his past had to be. There he found fists and boots and bushwhackers' lead, and as he breathed fire and gun-smoke and watched the dead pile up, there was still the final show-down to be faced . . .

Books by Hank J. Kirby in the Linford Western Library:

HELLFIRE PASS
BLOOD KIN

HANK J. KIRBY

TRAVIS QUINN, OUTLAW

Complete and Unabridged

LINFORD
Leicester

First published in Great Britain in 1999 by
Robert Hale Limited
London

First Linford Edition
published 2000
by arrangement with
Robert Hale Limited
London

British Library CIP Data

Kirby, Hank J.
Travis Quinn, outlaw.—Large print ed.—
Linford western library
1. Western stories
2. Large type books
I. Title
823.9′14 [F]

ISBN 0–7089–5632–7

Published by
F. A. Thorpe (Publishing) Ltd.
Anstey, Leicestershire

Set by Words & Graphics Ltd.
Anstey, Leicestershire
Printed and bound in Great Britain by
T. J. International Ltd., Padstow, Cornwall

This book is printed on acid-free paper

For Michael James
of
Jakarta—
Selemat Datan!

1

Stage to Oblivion

The morning was the clearest he could remember, fresh and crammed with the residual sparkle of last night's shower of rain. Jewels glinted on the damp leaves of trees, and the sun was a huge golden nugget as it dragged itself above the line of the hills.

There hadn't been enough rain to really lay the dust and the corral was shrouded in a ruby-tinged haze as Dave Callahan tossed his rope over the old palomino mare. She, too, sensed the exhilaration of the morning and played with him with unaccustomed friskiness for a seven-year-old. Callahan grinned as the animal reared, pawed the dusty air, tugged at the rope he held. He had no real trouble bringing the mare down to all four feet, and he patted the muzzle and twigged an ear lightly as the horse allowed him to back her into a corner. He threw on the faded Indian blanket and the weathered Denver saddle, reaching for the cinch strap. By then Claire was calling him from the cabin: breakfast was ready on this special day.

Claire bustled about, serving him an extra-large plate of bacon, eggs and beans, and a square of stale cornpone fried in the grease, just the way he liked it. The coffee was about as perfect as it could be, having been made from beans that had languished in the calico bag for nigh on six months. But they still held a mouth-watering aroma.

Young Donny crawled up into Callahan's lap and with all of a two-year-old's lack of consideration snatched the square of fried cornpone.

'Hey, you little tike! Gimme that!' But in the struggle the cornpone fell to the floor and the old yeller dog, Sally (where *had* that name come from anyway?), lazily stretched her neck and the morsel was gone in a gulp.

Callahan leaned back in his chair with a sigh and tousled the crestfallen Donny's dark curls. He winked at Claire. 'It's the thought that counts, so they say.'

She laughed — that warm, ringing sound that had echoed inside his skull since the moment they had first met.

She wasn't a very tall woman, coming to just below his shoulder — and he was a stringbean six-two in his socks when he wore any. This morning she had her straw-coloured hair loose about her shoulders, framing her oval face, the way he liked it. Again, he knew she had worn it this way to please him.

'I'll be having many thoughts until you return, Dave,' she said soberly. 'All about you.'

He lightly pinched her buttock and she twitched away, filly-like, admonishing him with a flushed look. 'Davey! The boy!'

'I Donny, not Day!'

Callahan dandled the child on his

knee, looking at his wife, reading the worry she tried to hide in her pale green eyes. 'I'll be back soon as I can, Claire — and we'll be on the way to riches.'

'Riches sound good, but you hurry back, Dave. I — I don't like you travelling when there are so many outlaws about these days.'

'These days, those days — there've always been outlaws, dear, always will be.'

'But there seem to have been so many hold-ups and robberies these past months! All very violent!'

He tugged at her skirt and drew her closer, the three of them in a small, tight-knit group now. 'The stage is only carrying passengers, Claire. No payrolls, no bullion, no strong-boxes. I'll be in Socorro by noon tomorrow. If Caswell has kept his word, he'll have the bulls ready. I'll pay him and start driving them back right away . . . I'll be home by the end of the week.'

She leaned down and lightly kissed the jet-black straight hair, saw the flash of pleasure in his dark eyes. 'That's the day I'll be looking for.'

He held up Donny's small, soft hand and began bending the chubby fingers and thumb, counting one to five as he did so, the boy chiming in belatedly, but happily.

'Five days — then start looking for my dust in the high pass over Patterson's Peak. You'll see it. You can count on it.'

She felt a surge in her chest at his casual confidence and, feeling a little foolish at her anxiety, leaned down and hugged both her men tightly.

'I know, Davey,' she said quietly, using that special endearment she usually reserved for their intimate moments. 'I know I can always count on you. I guess that's one of the nicest things about you — I can always depend on you.'

'Always,' he assured her.

The stage was due to leave at noon.

By sundown, Dave Callahan's life would have changed forever.

* * *

He was right about the stage not carrying valuables — there were no strong-boxes, no payroll satchels, no bank-bags of gold nuggets or cash. Just the driver, a regular armed guard — there was still the odd band of bloodthirsty reservation bucks running wild along the Socorro trail — and the five passengers. Dave Callahan, a bank clerk in a Derby hat that was one size too small and looked ridiculous sitting atop his thick thatch of silver hair; a woman who wore a lot of face paint and had a tough look about her, but she said little, reading from a leather-bound book that Callahan thought looked suspiciously like one of those pocket-size Bibles the missionaries were distributing to reservation Indians; another woman, mountainously fat, already perspiring profusely, waving a cheaply-scented handkerchief about her multichinned face; and, finally, a hard-eyed man with tobacco-stained longhorn moustaches whose shirt pocket was pierced by a series of small holes that might have been made by the prong of a law badge.

It seemed like an ordinary stage-load of passengers, and Callahan settled back, eased down in his seat, causing the fat lady to huff and puff away from him an extra inch or so, throwing him a dirty look in the process. He tilted his hat forward over his dark eyes, the brim resting on the rather large hawk-like nose, and covering most of his swarthy face.

Then the stage lurched and the driver cussed as he usually did when the team was slow to start. The fat lady *harumphed* loudly and he called down 'Sorry, ma'am!', without sounding in the least contrite. The battered old Concord rattled down the rutted main street and out over the small, arched wooden bridge that spanned Arrow

Creek, the watercourse which gave the town its name. No more than a trickle now, it would become a raging torrent come spring and the thawing of the snows on the mountains, particularly on Patterson's Peak.

It was ten after 1 p.m. when the stage cleared town — good going for that particular line, which had been known to be twenty-four hours behind schedule on more than one occasion.

No one on the walks or dusty street paid much attention to the battered coach as it swayed and creaked out of town: it really wasn't worth a second glance.

But that stage was about to be propelled into the legends of the South-West, and an infamy never expected, never even *considered*, by any of the citizens of Arrow Creek.

For while the stagecoach that day on the Socorro run might not have been carrying valuables or strong-boxes, one of its passengers was, clothes padded with thousands of dollars . . . They swayed along the dusty high trail through the Windrush Mountains, oblivious. But there were people who were mighty interested in that particular passenger, so much so that a band of hard-eyed, gun-hung men set out early to intercept the Concord. And the best place, of course, to do this was where the driver had his attention firmly fixed on the eight-in-hand team, as they rounded a hairpin bend above a sheer drop of a hundred feet into a blind canyon, known in that part of New Mexico simply as The Pit.

It was just on sundown, the shadows long.

They knew their stuff, these hard men, and they lost no time going about the kind of job they'd done a dozen times before.

The driver fought and cussed and sawed the team around the hairpin, standing in his seat, making a fine target for any lurking bushwhacker. But the bullet that smashed down from the ridge just around the bend wasn't aimed at him. It drove into the brain of the off-side lead horse — at about the same time as the second bullet, from behind a birch tree clinging to the mountainside above the trail, brought down the near-side leader.

The driver was pulled off-balance by the tight-held reins as the horses went down, thrashing, and the others rammed into them and each other as the stage swayed dangerously close to the edge.

The passengers tumbled in a tangled heap inside, the fat woman pinning a gasping Callahan to the floor, the bank clerk and the hard-eyed man Callahan suspected of being a lawman swearing and to hell with the fat lady's sensitivity. Only the painted lady with the small Bible made no sound, but she was very white underneath the rouge and eye-shadow. They all struggled, each hindering the others in their attempts to untangle themselves and see what the hell was going on.

By then, the Concord had slithered

to a stop, riding up over the downed team, leaning at a precarious angle. Dust swirled. The driver lay unconscious in the trail. The guard sat up awkwardly, dazed and bruised from his own fall. The injured horses were shrilling and whinnying, lucky that they hadn't busted their legs, though all of them had gashes or badly scraped hide.

Four men masked with bandannas covering the lower halves of their faces rode into the chaos, guns held in a threatening manner. The man on the dirty white horse, closest to the stage, heaved open the door and looked down into the struggling mass of people.

'Sorry about the rough stuff, folks, but there's one of you ain't quite what he seems . . . fact, he's totin' a heap of money sewed into his clothes. Someone figured it'd be a way of beatin' all these badmen who've been holdin' up the stages lately . . . '

He paused, and one or two of the other bandits laughed.

The one who had done all the talking

leaned into the coach, pushing the silent, painted woman to one side with a grunted apology. He tapped the pinned-down bank clerk with his rifle barrel. 'C'mon out, Vestey. You should never've volunteered for this chore. That mis'able old Banker Teasdale won't pay you no extra.'

The clerk was shaking — Callahan could feel him as he clambered over him — already lifting his hands. 'Don't hurt me! You — you can have the money . . . There's eleven thousand dollars . . . ' Vestey stumbled — and provided enough cover for the lawman to get out a hideaway gun and shoot into the outlaw's masked face. The man was smashed back, spilling from the saddle, the mask torn and already soaked with blood.

The others began shouting, and suddenly guns blasted angrily. The lawman dug an elbow into Callahan as he tried to get up. 'You got a gun, now's the time to use it!'

'I don't — pack a — gun!' gasped

Callahan. He couldn't even see what had happened for the mound of blubber crushing him against the floor.

But it was already too late.

The dead man's place had been taken by his three companions, crowding into the doorway, their guns roaring, spitting flame and death. They had already killed the driver and guard.

The noise inside the coach was deafening, drowning out the screams of the fat woman, the bleats of the bank clerk, the dying curses of the lawman. Callahan never got a chance to make any kind of a noise: there was a hammer-blow somewhere in his head and he left his part of the world in a blinding white flash.

The painted woman never made a sound as the bullets thudded into her twisting body.

* * *

There was still a lot of whiteness when he began to swim up out of the pitch blackness of oblivion. It hurt his eyes and he couldn't see beyond it — but he could hear a drone of quiet, though unintelligible, voices through the crashing in his head.

The whiteness dulled to grey and all the way to black again, then lightened back to grey and, after a long while, there was one last brief flare of white, like a swirling snowstorm that reminded him of his boyhood in the Black Hills of Dakota. Then it was dull yellow and the voices were clearer. He heard a man saying soberly, 'It's been five days, Claire, and he's been in and out of a coma all that time . . . Just — don't expect too much, my dear . . .'

'Oh, my God!' exclaimed a woman's voice, almost frantically. 'His eyes are open!'

Then she was leaning over him, straw hair spilling about her pale face, and he smelled her sweetness, felt her warm breath against his fevered face. 'Davey! Oh, my darling!'

He blinked but was still unable to see

her clearly, because she was so close. He said very clearly and not a little irritably, 'Will you stand back from me? Who are you, anyway? And, by the way, my name's not 'Davey'. It's Travis Quinn.' He struggled to sit up. 'And where the hell am I?'

2

Lone Survivor

'You were the only survivor,' Doc Fisher finished his story as he looked down at the blank-faced man who called himself 'Travis Quinn', lying bandaged and half-propped-up in the infirmary bed. 'No one's sure just what happened, but it seems the others had all been shot — and that's certainly a bullet wound along the side of your head.'

'No use asking me, Doc. I dunno what the hell you're talking about.' He flicked his dark eyes to the white-faced, red-eyed Claire Callahan sitting on the edge of a straight-back chair, hands clasped in her lap, holding a soggy handkerchief.

The man's dark eyes softened very slightly. 'Ma'am, I'm sorry. I — I meant no disrespect, but I just — don't know you. You've got me mixed-up with someone else.'

She stood abruptly. 'What a foolish thing to say! You've been married to me for just over three years! We have a son, Donny! Are you going to deny his existence, too?'

The doctor crossed to her and slid an arm about her shoulders, speaking quietly, but she pushed him aside impatiently, staring hard at the man in the bed.

'You're my *husband*!' she choked. 'David Callahan!'

He shook his bandaged head, wincing slightly. 'My name's Travis Quinn, ma'am. I'm from Dakota — the Black Hills to pin it down.'

Trembling, Claire curled a lip. 'Very likely! That's Indian country, isn't it?'

'Yes'm — I'm part Sioux, with a touch of Cheyenne, and more than a little Irish.'

Claire gasped, and allowed the doctor to ease her down in the chair again.

'You — why are you doing this, David? You come from Monroe Station, Louisiana. There is a small amount of Creole blood in you but — '

She broke off at the look on his face. Then she put a trembling hand to her mouth and buried her face in the damp handkerchief. The man calling himself Quinn looked towards the doctor, rubbing gently at his throbbing head.

'Doc — I don't know you. I don't know this town . . . '

'Arrow Creek, New Mexico.'

Quinn shook his head slowly. 'I — I know my name is Travis Quinn, and I have Indian blood, just as I said a minute ago. I just don't know this lady . . . She says we're married, but that can't be . . . ' He paused and added, frowning, 'I already have a wife, named Rachel, and far as I know, she's waiting for me in Cheyenne, Wyoming.'

The doctor glanced at Claire: she had snapped her head up at Quinn's words, her face twisting in horror. But all she did was shake her head slowly in total disbelief.

'What I'm doing in New Mexico, I have no idea,' Quinn added, 'but I sure do have one helluva headache and my vision ain't any too sharp.'

The doctor examined him carefully, spending time looking into his eyes and the dark, dilated pupils. He stood back slowly, the elbow of his right arm cupped in his left hand, at waist level, his lips pursed thoughtfully.

'There's no doubt in my mind you are suffering from concussion — you were covered in blood when they found you in that bullet-riddled stagecoach. Everyone thought you were dead, but it seems it was mostly the blood of the other passengers. You were on the bottom, beneath the other bodies, so that probably saved you from taking more than the single bullet in the head. It was all lopsided when I first saw you, swollen with oedema.'

'Whatever the hell that is.'

'A swelling, as I said, usually

associated with excess fluid, the body's way of cushioning damage to an organ. I drew it off with a hypodermic but now I'm wondering if . . .'

Quinn spoke impatiently as the doctor paused. 'Wonderin' what, doc? You gonna tell me I've lost my memory?'

The doctor arched his eyebrows. 'You're familiar with amnesia?'

'Saw a couple fellers during the war who had it — temporarily. They both regained their memory after a while.'

'Yes, sometimes that happens if the initial memory loss wasn't too traumatic, or too great. No, I wasn't going to say you've *lost* your memory. I was going to say that, rather, you've *regained* it . . . '

Quinn stared, frowning, trying to take that in.

The woman stopped crying, wiped her eyes, absently blew her nose. Both of them stared blankly at the doctor who seemed to be holding down some rising excitement.

Quinn said, 'You've lost me, Doc.'

The doctor tugged at an earlobe. 'You're adamant that your real name is Travis Quinn?'

'Damn right I am!'

'You never used to curse,' Claire said in a strained voice and he looked at her, those bleak eyes softening slightly as before. He swivelled his gaze to the medic.

'You sound very much as if you — belong — to the Quinn name . . . It's not as if you just snatched it out of the air when you opened your eyes. You *knew* the name well.'

'Ought to. It's been mine for thirty-some years.'

'But not the last three years!' Claire said shortly, and the doctor raised a placating hand towards her.

'Just a moment, Claire — what I want you both to consider is this. Suppose 'David Callahan' was an assumed name. Probably not in any deliberate attempt to confuse, but — a name you made up, Mr Quinn

— simply because you couldn't recall your real name.'

There was a silence in the room. Heavy. Electric.

'I, too, saw many head-wounds during the war, Mr Quinn. I was fascinated by those men whose memories were affected by them. It's an area of which we are mainly ignorant in the medical profession, but progress is being made and I've tried to keep abreast of the latest findings — '

He sighed, took out a bent-stem pipe, absently poked a dark-stained thumb into the empty bowl, sucked on the stem.

'What I'm trying to say is that when you arrived in Arrow Creek, or perhaps for some time before that, you had already lost your memory — and forgotten your name, of course. So you became 'David Callahan'.'

'Doc,' Quinn said slowly. 'You're making my headache worse.'

'I'm sorry — I'll be brief.' He pointed towards Quinn's bandaged head. 'Just under your hairline towards the left front, there's a rather deep starshaped scar. You had this when you arrived in Arrow Creck. You'd had a fall from a horse and hit your head on a rock, you told me. But you were vague about details and where it had happened and where you were from . . . I believe that wound caused pressure on that part of your brain and affected your memory. Now this bullet wound . . . although it's further to the side and higher than the other scar, the shock of the lead striking your skull may well have caused the pressure to ease — and with my draining away the fluid, your real memory returned. In part, anyway.'

'Just like that?' Quinn tried to snap his fingers but was too weak.

'You've been comatose for five days, sir, so, no, not 'just like that', I'm afraid.'

Both men looked towards Claire. She was barely recognizable as the sweet-faced woman Doc Fisher had known for many years. She seemed — broken, was the most suitable word he could think of.

'You — you realize you've just shattered my life, Doctor?' she whispered hoarsely, her trembling mouth starting to tighten.

She flinched as he reached to lay a comforting hand on her shoulder. 'I'm sorry, my dear — it's no one's doing. It's simply — fate, for want of a better word.'

'Damn your words!' she hissed, eyes a little wild now as they rested on Quinn. 'Damn you — both!'

* * *

During the next few weeks, the man calling himself Travis Quinn had many visitors — Arrow Creek folk who claimed to know him — as David Callahan, of course. The barber, the livery man, two barkeeps from the Strongbow saloon, a couple of cowpunchers from ranches outside of town, the stage company manager, some lady friends of Claire's — and the Arrow Creek sheriff, Bud Hardiman.

He was a man about Quinn's age and had been lawman in Arrow Creek for seven years. He was tough when he had to be, kind in a gruff way when he decided there was no need to bend a gun barrel over a man's head, but he was a stubborn man, too. He never forgot a hurt, positively hated wild-ass cowpunchers who stopped by with trail herds and figured they could shoot the small town to pieces and to hell with the safety of its citizens. Bud Hardiman wouldn't stand for that kind of behaviour and many a ranny nursing a hangover also had a spate of bruises and even some broken bones to nurse as well, when he was kicked beyond the town limits the morning after a wild night amongst the fleshpots of Arrow Creek.

As for outlaws who robbed and killed, Hardiman had a consuming hatred for such men and their deeds. And he was determined to learn what had happened to that stagecoach on the Socorro run where everyone was slaughtered in cold blood — everyone but Dave Callahan.

Or Travis Quinn as he insisted he was now.

That name bothered Hardiman some: he had heard it somewhere, years ago maybe, but it was sitting in a dark corner of his mind and he knew sooner or later he would drag it out into the light . . . For now, he visited Quinn as often as he could and, despite the doctor's assurance that the man would have absolutely no memory of what had happened on that stage, he questioned Quinn relentlessly on the subject.

'Judas, Sheriff! Don't you think I *want* to remember?'

Bud Hardiman had a long, horse-like face and he scratched at his heavy jaw as he faced Quinn unsmilingly. 'I dunno as I do, *amigo*. You rode out on that stage as Dave Callahan, respected rancher, with a wife and son — Now you ride back denyin' their existence. I ain't a real smart man. I just don't savvy it, is all.'

'That makes two of us, Sheriff. But it seems I was shot with the others, but, being on the bottom of the pile, with them bleeding all over me, I guess the robbers must've figured I was dead.'

Hardiman's eyes narrowed. 'You recollect that? Bein' under the pile of bodies?'

'No! Doc Fisher told me that's what happened.'

'He did, huh?' The sheriff sounded sceptical.

Quinn was wearing a single, narrow bandage about his head now and it bunched up his hair, giving his face a longer, narrower look than was usual. 'You and me get along okay when you knew me as Dave Callahan, Hardiman?'

'I still know you as Callahan! Yeah, we got along okay, you never made me no trouble — But I always figured you was a mite too quiet, hardly ever cussed, didn't drink much — and never toted a gun.' He leaned forward quickly at the look on Quinn's face. 'You recollect somethin'?'

'No-ooo — Just that I always carry a six-gun, a rifle, too . . . It's something I — *need* to do. Don't ask me why . . . '

'Gunfighter?' Hardiman spoke the word half aloud, as if asking himself the question. Was *that* why the name Travis Quinn stirred something way back in his memory? *A gunfighter — a hardcase* . . .

'Why'd anyone hold up the stage?' Quinn asked abruptly. 'I mean, Doc said it wasn't carrying valuables.'

The lawman scowled. 'It wasn't, but the banker figured to play it smart, had one of his clerks sew eleven thousand bucks into his clothes — '

Quinn pursed his lips. 'And someone blabbed.'

'Yeah — I've narrowed it down to two of the bank's staff — I'll know which one by tonight. Then I'll find out who he talked to.' Hardiman stood.

'Dave — Mister — I don't like bein' made a fool of, so you got any notion of doin' that, think about it mighty careful before you go ahead and does it. OK? I'll be back.'

Quinn rubbed gently at his throbbing head as the door closed behind the sheriff. It opened seconds later and a worried-looking Doc Fisher entered. He went straight to Quinn, lifted his wrist and took his pulse.

'Sheriff's a hard man to stop — I've asked him not to bother you so much . . . '

'I can handle him, I guess, Doc — But I tell you, I'm mightily confused. I mean, I *know* my name is Travis Quinn. I have a wife named Rachel in Cheyenne — but I — I've got other things running round my mind like a millwheel . . . '

'It may even get more confusing before it gets better, I'm afraid,' the doctor said slowly. 'You may mix things up, believe wholeheartedly that something is just so and it could turn out to be entirely wrong — confusion and half-truths are all a part of regaining your memory, Travis. The thing is, don't let all the disappointments sink you into depression. That will only delay, even prevent, complete recovery of your memory . . . D'you recall any people? Places?'

'Faces, but can't put names to 'em . . . and the word 'Alamosa' . . . Mean anything to you, Doc?'

'Believe there's a town called Alamosa in Colorado — on the Rio Grande in the San Luis Valley . . . '

Yes! By God, that sounded right! Quinn still had no clear picture but he *knew* something had happened there, something he had to find out about . . .

* * *

Two days later, Bud Hardiman came hurrying into the infirmary, face grim. He stopped dead when he saw the doctor standing beside the empty bed.

'Where's Quinn?'

'Gone, Bud — during the night, I guess.' He waved a piece of paper. 'Left me an IOU pinned to the pillow.'

Hardiman frowned. 'He fit to ride?'

'I don't see why not. He's fit physically. It's his mental state I'm concerned with — he's still very confused and it could land him in a lot of trouble.'

The sheriff snorted, dug into his jacket pocket and handed the medic a large fold of paper. 'He's already in trouble, Doc. I figure he run out because he knew I'd find out about him sooner or later . . . Take a look, Doc.'

The paper was a yellowed Wanted dodger. It bore a crude likeness of Travis Quinn beneath the words, 'REWARD $5,000.'

In smaller type beneath the picture:

Travis Quinn — Outlaw
Wanted for Rustling and
Armed Robbery
Caution —
This Man Is Dangerous!

3

Danger Man!

During the night, Claire Callahan heard a sound out in the yard. She snapped her eyes open, lying stiffly in the bed: she hadn't been able to sleep since they'd brought in Dave from the stage wreck . . . She instinctively glanced towards the cot where Donny was sleeping peacefully, then sucked in a sharp breath as she heard the sound outside again.

Something was disturbing the horses in the corral.

She slid out from beneath the sheet, parted the curtains and looked out. There was a half moon but the sky was overcast and all she could see was a moving shadow amongst the horses. At first she thought it was some animal. But, no!

It was more like a crouching man with a rope . . .

She lost no time in throwing on a gown and, heart hammering, hurried through to the parlour and took down the single-barrelled Ithaca shotgun from the wall rack. She fumbled out some shells from a drawer in a bureau and dropped the first on the floor in her hurry to load. Dave would never allow a loaded gun in the house, she thought, thrusting the shell home finally.

She swallowed, flung open the door and stepped out onto the porch.

'Get away from my horses or I'll shoot!' She was pleased that her voice didn't sound shaky and saw the shadow straighten, turn towards her.

'Ma'am, I mean no harm. It's Travis Quinn.'

Claire reeled: that was the last thing she expected to hear. She was still dazed, the shotgun waving wildly as she clung one-handed to the rail.

By that time, he was at the steps, came up in one bound and roughly took the weapon from her. 'Ma'am, you never even cocked the hammer . . . Now, if I'd been someone up to no good . . . '

She faced him, hands clenched at her sides. 'Just *what* are you up to? And I refuse to say the name you are using now! You are still Dave Callahan to me!'

He sighed. She saw him move his feet to steady himself, and realized he wasn't as spry as he'd tried to appear. She frowned. 'Aren't you supposed to be in the infirmary still?'

'Had enough of confinement, ma'am . . . '

'Can't you at least bring yourself to use *my* name? Claire is *my* real one, you know.'

He stood the gun against the wall. 'Claire — I'm truly sorry about everything. I've tried until I've just about sweated blood but I — still can't recollect you.' He held up a hand swiftly as she started to retort. 'Believe me, it's no trick, no act, nothing intentional — my memory just don't carry anything about — you . . .'

'Oh, dear God!' she breathed and her voice shook now. She stepped back quickly as he reached for her wrist. 'Don't touch me! Not until you — remember me!'

His teeth flashed briefly as he smiled faintly. 'Careful — that's as close as dammit to an admission you believe me.'

'I find nothing whatsoever humorous in this situation! And you still haven't told me what you're doing here . . . And how did you find this place — if you can't remember!'

'Claire — you told me so many times how to get here when you visited me in the infirmary. Doc Fisher did, too . . . 'Use the trail that takes you through the high pass on Patterson's Peak'. Well, I can read and there are a couple of signs . . . I stole a horse from the doc's stable, left him an IOU. But it's a harness hoss — I need something I can travel on.'

'And you expect me to give you such a mount?'

He stared at her for a long time, her face mostly shadowed. 'If I really *am* Dave Callahan, aren't they my own horses?'

She stiffened and he could see plainly how her mouth tightened.

'Oh, so now you're being smart, are you? What else do you expect? Money? I mean, using your logic, whatever money I have in the cabin is really yours anyway . . . even if you don't wish to admit to your true identity!'

'Claire, I savvy how you must feel . . . '

'Oh, *do* you! And I wonder just how you accomplished that miracle!'

He moved his hands helplessly. 'Look, I'm going north. I have a memory of a town up there but I'm not sure how I got there or why . . . I need to find out what happened to me. Far as I'm concerned I'm Travis Quinn, and my wife Rachel is back in Cheyenne, Wyoming. You say I'm this Dave

Callahan, your husband, father of your child . . . I'd reckon you'd be interested in knowing the straight of it, too.'

There was a silence between them then. The horses snorted and stomped a little. Distantly, some nightbird called down by the creek. A fish plopped.

Claire, shaking, pulled her gown tighter across her body. When she spoke, he could hardly hear her.

'All right — I — suppose it's only right I should — well, I admit I'm a little afraid of — learning the truth.'

'Me, too,' he said quietly, surprising her.

She almost smiled for a moment. 'But you really have no idea what this has done to me!'

'Don't get the notion that I'm in anyways happy, either, Claire! I had a life that was busted-up, too. Maybe two lives . . . '

She nodded. 'Take whatever horse you want — your favourite was the palomino but she's too old for what you want to do now. Try the buckskin gelding. And that big sorrel, if you want a spare. I — I'll make you up a grubsack.'

He thanked her and roped the horses, found a saddle in the barn and returned to the porch where she now waited. She indicated the sack of food, and handed him some money.

'There's forty dollars there — it's about half of what we had in the cookie jar but I — I need something to live on. You had a rifle you kept for hunting up in the attic. Your 'yellowboy' you called it.'

'The good old brass-action Winchester '66,' he said, sounding pleased. 'I'll leave it with you, I guess. You may need it.'

She hesitated, reached out and laid a trembling hand on his arm. 'Perhaps one day, you'll — come back for it?'

He covered her hand with his and squeezed. 'I'll be back whatever I find out — I reckon I owe you that much, Claire.' He gestured to distant Patterson's Peak, the snowcap glinting dully like silver in the night. 'Watch for my dust in the high pass.'

She stiffened and snatched her hand away, and he heard her suck in a sharp breath.

'I'm sorry — did I say something to upset you?'

She shook her head but it was a short time before she replied. 'It's what Dave always said to me when he was going to town or to Socorro to buy cattle . . . 'Watch for my dust in the high pass across Patterson's Peak . . .'.'

'Well, it just seemed like a — natural thing to say. It just came out.'

This time she did smile. Only briefly, but suddenly she felt better.

Whoever this man really was, he had just touched something they had shared — accidentally, maybe, but it gave her hope.

And the Good Lord knew she hadn't had much of that these past weeks . . .

* * *

Albuquerque was where he first struck trouble.

It had been a long, tiring ride up from Arrow Creek and he had instinctively kept to the wild trails. More and more memories were coming back but there was a kind of strange unreality about them.

He was *sure* his name was Travis Quinn — but the other things he recalled, about places and people and incidents, well, they were real enough and yet there was some feeling that, although they had happened to him, there was something not quite right about them.

He couldn't explain it and he had a nervous, edgy feeling that kept him awake and had him swivelling his head every few minutes in the saddle, jumping at every wilderness sound. Travelling unarmed was likely a basic cause of this and he aimed to do something about that just as soon as he was able.

This meant hitting a town and some

deep instinct told him to stay clear of towns for now. He had no idea why, but a hunch warned him and he heeded it. Claire Callahan had packed him plenty of grub and extra clothing, and what he could trap for himself along the trail kept him tolerably well-fed. Water was no problem, following the trail that he did, and he marvelled that he was able to locate hidden Indian springs in some places, figured he must have known about this source of water long ago.

After a bear caught him off-guard and chased him and the two mounts downhill in the Manzanas Mountains, claw-marking the sorrel on the rump, Quinn figured that was enough: he had to have a gun, a rifle if possible, certainly a Peacemaker in any case.

Guns cost money and he had little enough to take him to Alamosa — and beyond. For he still kept thinking about Rachel in Cheyenne. A golden-skinned, raven-haired woman whose beauty had always intrigued him. She could have heen part-Indian but she had told him no, her ancestors came from the Mediterranean. Why could he recall such small details and not other, more important, ones? He couldn't even remember the wedding . . .

But he shook off such thoughts as he rode down out of the hills — they came to him unbidden each night and he was determined they would not distract him during the day, too.

Albuquerque was his goal. As he remembered it, there was a gunsmith in a back street called Marsden or something like that — *Gedsen*! That was it! Yeah, a shifty type who asked no questions, could make up a man exactly what he wanted in the way of firearms. Of course, he charged like hell for doing it but — well, forty bucks wouldn't even be enough to have him reaching for his gun-making kit, so he would have to take a different approach.

He timed it so that he rode into town just after dark, worked his way around the streets until he found the one he wanted. Deaf Man Lane.

There was a light burning at the back of Gadsen's shop, the windows just as grimy as Quinn remembered, the signs faded, merely saying 'Gunsmithing — Cheap Rates For Top Work'. Half the letters were gone but Gadsen preferred it that way.

Quinn looked about him, saw a movement in some shadows and a man shuffled out, fumbling at his trousers' front, staggering as he headed back towards the main drag and no doubt the saloons or cat-houses there, waiting to strip him of whatever money he still had in his pockets.

He had to rap hard and shake the door in its frame before he saw light sweep across the windows from inside, and then the door opened part-way, on a chain. A lantern was held high — Gadsen had it at arm's length, standing to one side.

Quinn smiled: he hadn't changed much. Ratsmart as ever. 'Need to do a deal for some guns, Gad.'

There was a brief silence and Quinn couldn't be quite sure if he heard a sharp in-sucking of breath or not. Then a coarse, phlegmy voice said,

'I know you?'

'Once you did — and I paid well.'

Part of a squarish face was washed by the weak light, showing the scarred nose Gadsen had earned when trying to cheat a notorious gunman on a custom-made rifle. He was lucky he was still alive — but the word was that he had got a message to the nearest marshal and the gunman had been ambushed along the Santa Fe Trail. He'd chosen to fight it out and the marshal's posse had blown him apart with their withering volley of fire.

It was said the reward money had helped furnish new gun-making lathes for Gadsen.

'By God, I *thought* it was you! Man, you're s'posed to be dead!'

That shook Quinn a little but he just shrugged and said, 'As you can see, I'm not — now open up.'

'Nah, I don't think so. You always were trouble. Sure, you paid okay, but I can do without the kinda trouble you bring. Sorry.'

Quinn's boot jammed in the door as the gunsmith tried to close it. 'Gad — you better let me in. Or call the town fire station, because you're gonna need 'em.'

Gadsen swore, hesitated a little longer, then unlatched the door. He hurried through to the back, leaving the door for Quinn to see to. When he walked into the lighted parlour where Gadsen had been having a meal, the man was waiting, holding a big Le Mat revolver, the hammer cocked, the barrel-mouths yawning. The top barrel fired a .40-calibre ball and there were nine chambers in the thick cylinder to feed it. The second, underslung barrel yawned to a massive .62-calibre and also fired a twenty-gauge shotshell.

Gadsen grinned crookedly as he saw Quinn stop dead in his tracks. 'Originally a percussion pistol as you know, but I've converted it to cartridge — nine in .44-calibre, and a shotshell full of 20-gauge buckshot from the under-barrel — Now — if you was plannin' somethin' froggy . . .'

Quinn lifted his hands just above waist level. 'Told you, Gad — need to do a deal. No need for this kinda greeting.'

Gadsen was a man in his early fifties, thick-necked, with powerful shoulders and hands. He was six inches shorter than Quinn but, whether he held a gun or not, he was a dangerous man. That was why he had survived for so long in his trade.

'You shouldn't be here, Quinn.'

'Just passin' through. Not looking for trouble, just some guns — rifle and pistol.' He gestured to the huge Le Mat. 'That would be nice . . .'

Gadsen laughed. 'Bet it would! But you ain't got enough money to buy this!'

'I'll settle for a tuned Peacemaker and a Winchester.'

'Yallerboy in .44/.40? That was your style, weren't it?'

Quinn frowned, remembering Claire had told him his hunting rifle — as Dave Callahan — had been a Winchester '66 with a brass action, the well-known 'Yellowboy' Winchester.

'Well, what can you do for me, Gad? I don't have a lot of time.'

'On the run?'

'No — just impatient to get where I'm going.'

'And where would that be?'

'Forget it — just fix me up with some weapons and I'll trade you a big buckskin in damn good shape.'

'Hell, I don't need another horse.'

'All I've got to offer — 'less you want to take a sorrel with grizzly clawmarks on one side of his rump.'

'So you come over the mountains,' Gadsen said, his mind instantly associating bears with Quinn's other information. 'I reckon you *are* on the run . . . '

Quinn seemed as if he would say

something, swayed and put a hand quickly to his head. He knocked off his hat and Gadsen squinted in surprise at the narrow bandage around his head.

'Hell, you been hurt . . . '

Quinn used those few seconds. While Gadsen was still surprised, he staggered a little closer and suddenly his left hand, holding the hat he had deliberately knocked off his head, swung in a savage arc.

The stiff felt slammed into the big Le Mat and although it weighed nearly four pounds, it partly fell from Gadsen's grip. Before the gunsmith could tighten up on it, Quinn drove his right fist against the man's square jaw, turning his head violently, sending him crashing into the wall. He took a long step forward and smashed his fist down on Gadsen's rising gunhand. The Le Mat thudded to the floor, in fact, right onto Gadsen's slippered foot and the man howled in pain, danced on one foot as he reached down awkwardly — but suddenly spun and rammed his bullet head into the oncoming Quinn's midriff.

Quinn grunted and felt the thick, muscular arms go about him, clamp tightly, thumb knuckles gouging across his kidney area. He gasped and felt the pressure surge in his head. He locked both hands together, lifted them above Gadsen's bent back and slammed them down on the man's spine several times. The last two blows drove Gadsen to his knees and Quinn lifted his own knee into the man's face. Blood spurted from nostrils and lips and Gadsen roared as he hurled himself away.

He dived for the heavy revolver but Quinn's boot heel crushed his little finger, and he rolled into the tall man's legs, sending him staggering. Gadsen came up fast, bloody-faced, wild-eyed, big fists swinging.

Quinn blocked the first blow and thought his arm was broken, it hit his forearm with such force. He stumbled back, side-stepped into a chair, grabbed at it for support. Then he swung it around and Gadsen jerked his head out of the way. But one leg splintered against his temple and he stumbled to one knee again.

Quinn lifted the chair above his head and brought it down viciously. The wood shattered and the gunsmith spread out on his face on the floor. He groaned and made as if to push erect. Quinn kicked him in the side of the head and he was still.

Breathing hard, Quinn pumped water into the zinc-lined sink in the kitchen, washed the blood from his face, wincing as it stung fresh cuts. He dried up on a rag of a towel, went back into the parlour. Gadsen hadn't moved.

Quinn picked up the heavy Le Mat and went through the door he knew led to the man's workshop. It smelled of metal shavings, oil and sawdust, with an underlying odour of gun powder. Lathes, vices and clamps glittered dully in the lamp light. Rifling rods stood in a bundle like fishing poles. Files, punches, taps and dies were scattered about, along with lead-headed hammers, sandpaper and swageing gear for the cartridges Gadsen sometimes handloaded.

Behind it all was a row of pigeon holes with weapons in it, some for repair, some half-assembled, some finished.

Quinn chose a Colt Frontier with a good balance and a smooth hammer action. There were plenty of oiled holster rigs to choose from. He loaded the Colt, filled the loops on his bullet belt, and dropped half-a-dozen cartons of ammunition into an empty calico coffee-bean bag. There was no Yellowboy rifle, but he found a blued-action '73 that was smooth as a highclass whore's silk stockings. It was the same calibre as his Colt.

He unloaded the massive Le Mat, deciding the weapon was too large for man-carry. It would be a fine saddle gun and had, in fact, been designed for that purpose, but it would weigh a man down if he tried to hang its four pounds of iron on his belt.

Gadsen was half-conscious when he got back to the parlour. Quinn shook him, ignoring the man's moans, held up the guns and the bag of ammunition. 'I'll leave the buckskin tied to your fence.'

Gadsen squinted, his eyes pain-filled. 'Son of a bitch! Never did like you, Quinn! Never did!'

'Mutual, Gad — by the by, you remember that feller I ran with for a spell? Kidder — and he had a sidekick — Stroud, if I recollect . . .'

Gadsen merely looked, sniffing, wiping his blood-dripping nose.

'Know where I can find 'em? Need to get in touch.'

Gadsen snorted, spat some blood on the floor. 'Not Stroud you won't — Billy-Jack Kaye backshot him in La Plata last year — Stroud raped Billy's woman. Where the hell you been?'

Quinn shrugged. 'Down south.'

'Yeah — figured you musta been south of the Rio to hide out good enough to make folk think you was dead . . . The hell you come back for?'

Quinn played a hunch. 'The hell you think?'

Gadsen stared at him, then smiled, broken teeth showing bloodily behind his split lips. 'Yeah, you was always a mean one when someone crossed you. Well, Stew Kidder won't be easy to get to, you know that. Fact, he kinda upset the law some around Catamount, up in Colorado — reckon he went deeper into the Wolfpacks than any white man's ever been.'

'Well, if you're an outlaw and every man's hand's turned agin you, Gad, the only place to go is where others ain't game to go.'

'Well, I reckon you'd know. All right, Quinn. Vamoose. I'll take the hoss, an' if he ain't good as you say, I'll pick up the difference some other time — you can bet on that.'

Quinn nodded with a crooked smile. 'I just know I can, Gad. Could've saved yourself a beating, you know.'

Gadsen said nothing, looking more shifty than ever. Quinn frowned slightly, then went out into the night.

As the door closed behind him, he heard Gadsen's muffled voice say viciously, 'I hope Daddow gutshoots you!'

Daddow! Another name . . . Another memory stirring . . .

4

Keep Ridin'!!

Claire Callahan waved the old Wanted dodger Sheriff Bud Hardiman had given her to read.

'I don't believe this!'

'Look for yourself, ma'am,' the lawman said wearily. 'It sure looks like your husband, and he was the one said his name was Travis Quinn.'

'But he's no outlaw! Why would he use 'Quinn' if he was?'

The sheriff said nothing, but his face was set in hard lines and it was clear he didn't aim to argue the point.

'Why would he have left an IOU for Doc Fisher if he was an outlaw?' she demanded.

Hardiman smiled faintly. 'So you've

seen him — figured he might ride out this way.'

Claire frowned, annoyed at her unconscious admission. 'Well, it's still his home, whatever name he chooses to go by!'

'Best tell me where he was headed, ma'am — you'll only be obstructin' the law otherwise and I figure you got enough trouble now without makin' more for yourself.'

She looked the sheriff straight in the eye. 'I don't know where he was going — we — aren't exactly friendly at this time.'

He took the dodger and held it up. 'You were quick to defend him.'

She sighed. 'Why not? I've been married to the man for more than three years. He's *never* shown any dishonest tendencies — why should I believe an old reward poster?'

'Old or not, that's his likeness . . . '

'Perhaps you should check and see if the reward's already been collected, Sheriff.' She said it stiffly, accusing. By the sly way he flicked his gaze away she knew she was right: Hardiman had his eye on the dollars . . .

'There's Donny awake — you'll have to excuse me, Sheriff.'

'Which direction did he go?' insisted Hardiman, but she feigned not to hear him and hurried into the house.

The sheriff hesitated, then swore under his breath, mounted up and rode out of the ranch yard. Sure, he'd like to get his hands on some of that five thousand . . . Maybe he'd just hole-up in the timber on the slopes for a spell. See if she was lying, and was still in touch with him . . .

Upstairs, at the bedroom window, Claire soothed the child who was only half-awake, rocking him in her arms, feeling him relax into sleep again.

She peered through the curtains and smiled faintly, seeing Hardiman's elaborately obvious exit, knowing he was going to be watching her for a day or so.

It wouldn't matter: she had no idea

where Dave Callahan was going.

But her eyes drifted to the distant high pass on Patterson's Peak.

Maybe one day she would see his dust up there, just before he started down the trail to the ranch. *Coming home* . . .

Maybe . . .

⋆ ⋆ ⋆

Travis Quinn was a long way from Patterson's Peak.

He had crossed from New Mexico into Colorado and was skirting La Jara at the southern end of the San Luis Valley. He would be in Alamosa the following morning with a little luck and effort on the part of the sorrel.

The horse's bear-wounds had healed well although it couldn't travel for long without limping and favouring the clawed hip. Quinn was a good man with horses, never flogged them to exhaustion, cared for the animals he depended on to carry him where he wanted to go. He had used natural poultices from wild herbs to hasten the healing of the wounds and had, in fact, used the same poultice source on the bullet gouge on his head. It was healing over now and his headaches were diminishing, his sight as sharp as it had ever been.

He had surprised himself, though, when he had tried his gun speed. It was still tolerable, and would get him out of most trouble he might have to face, but it was way slower than he wanted — he was reluctant to think 'as he *remembered*', for he still wasn't clear in his mind about some things. The memories seemed to be mixed-up in some way and he wondered if he was overlapping with other memories from the time when he had been 'Dave Callahan'. What was he really — cowman or gunslinger?

It was sure a strange thing, the human mind, and, in truth, it scared him a little, gave him a feeling of being not quite in control of himself . . .

But he hoped to find a few answers in Alamosa. Or, more particularly, just outside of the town, for he had recalled a small cabin out there on a grassy bench overlooking a creek that fed into the Rio Grande . . .

But he would stop in town first.

And that was a mistake.

As soon as he saw the town with its rambling streets and scattered buildings, he recognized it. This was a long, fertile valley, rich green showing far beyond the town, timber thick on the rising slopes of a low line of hills.

He made his way unerringly to the livery, stopped the weary sorrel at the horse-trough under a shady tree and allowed the animal to drink. He hooked a boot heel over the saddle horn and began to roll a cigarette. Folk looked at him with passing curiosity and he had smoked the cigarette halfway down before an unfriendly voice said, 'Keep ridin', Quinn — you were warned never to come back here. Gadsen wired to say you might try it though.'

The speaker was a well-dressed man, dark corduroy trousers tucked into half-boots, a light grey shirt that fitted a muscular torso much better than the usual gear stocked in frontier stores. His hat was unstained, and sported a snakeskin band. He was a man about Quinn's age, hard-eyed, lantern-jawed.

The gun rig about his waist was polished and supple, the Colt itself resting snugly in the holster which had two silver conches on the bands holding the main sheath to the heavier leather backing. The man's right hand rested lightly against this rig and Travis Quinn looked down into the cold blue eyes, set a little too closely so that they spoiled his looks. Except for the eyes, he could have been called handsome by some . . . Names flashed into Quinn's head, startling him.

'Still walking around, Daddow?' Quinn said, the name sliding easily into his mind to match up with the man.

'Figured you might've met your match by now.'

'No one faster's called me out, Quinn . . . not yet. And I know it won't be you.'

Quinn shrugged. 'Maybe one day we'll find out. Still got the same boss?'

'Mr Bannister pays my wages if that's what you mean — but I don't aim to stand in the sun jawing with the likes of you. Just keep ridin' like I said.'

Quinn flicked his cigarette and Marvin Daddow stepped back quickly, a cloud coming behind those icy eyes. Other men who had started to gather, looked a mite leery — as if they were expecting a confrontation that could result in gunsmoke and blood.

'Just get the hell outta Alamosa, before I forget myself and blow you outta that saddle!' gritted Daddow, right hand clamped around the stag handle of his Colt now.

Quinn unhooked his leg from the saddle horn and set his boot in the stirrup. 'Figured I might have a word with Bannister.'

'*Mister* Bannister's too busy to bother about you right now — you'd haveta get past me first, anyway.' He smiled thinly.

'Yeah, well, it ain't that important . . . I'll just buy me a few more stores and some feed for my hoss and . . . '

'No.' Daddow spoke quietly, so quietly that everyone gathered around heard the brief whisper as his gun cleared leather. The hammer was notched all the way back when the barrel settled steadily on Quinn. 'Just ride on through — plenty of grass and water in the valley — if that's where you're headed. If not . . . ' He shrugged indifferently.

'You're pushin', Daddow. And that's far enough.'

Quinn held the man's cold stare a long moment, then, not getting an answer from the hardcase, hauled the sorrel's head around and rode across the plaza towards the street that would take him out to the valley trail.

He lifted his gaze and smiled thinly: just as he had expected, Marv Daddow had back-up. Three rifles, or maybe only two and a shotgun, covered him from the roofs of false-front buildings as he rode slowly down the street.

He didn't look back, just rode on out of town and hit the valley trail for a mile or so. Then he cut away suddenly, riding up the middle of a stream, not leaving the water for more than half a mile. Then he chose a flat rocky place, left a couple of hoofprints for when they tracked him, rode back into the stream and continued on up for another mile before the water started to lap the sorrel's chest.

He went up a steep, brush-clad bank which hid his tracks, touched his spurs lightly to the weary mount, and rode into timber.

By sundown he came out above the grassy bench and there was the long, log-sided, sod-roofed cabin he remembered.

There were lights burning down there. Laughter, too. And singing. Drunken singing.

He eased down through the brush, sat the sorrel in shadow and watched. Four men, he could see. Boozing it up, passing around a stone jug of apple-jack or some kind of rot-gut.

They looked like cowmen and he glanced at the corrals, saw there was a dozen or so working mounts penned-up.

He nodded to himself. Somehow he had been kind of expecting this as he drew closer to the valley — and after meeting Daddow in Alamosa, he wasn't in the least surprised.

He knew what had happened. He'd seen the cattle on his way out here, cattle on range that used to be his, but was now under Bannister's B-Five brand.

'The son of a bitch just moved in!' he told himself quietly. 'Well, he always said he would . . . '

He unsheathed the Winchester and

levered in a fresh shell, as two of the drunken men grappled and rolled down a slope. The other two cheered them on. They looked filthy and unshaven in the yellow light spilling through the cabin door.

As one man lifted the stone jug to his mouth, Quinn shot it out of his hand. The jug exploded and the man reared away, hands and face bloody, dripping with whatever fire-water the vessel had contained.

His companion blinked, swayed, looking stupidly at the man beside him. The two fighters, sprawled on the grass, stopped their punching and gouging, looked towards the brush as Quinn kneed the sorrel into the open.

He let the rifle barrel move around, covering each in turn, walked the horse under their bleary gazes up to the door of the cabin. He stooped a little to look through the doorway and the man who had been cut by the exploding jug swore and grabbed at his holstered six-gun. He was pretty damn fast for a regular cow-hand but Quinn knew these weren't really cow-hands: they were hardcases, put in here by Bannister to hold the cabin — likely using it as a line camp now for B-Five.

Quinn swung the rifle one-handed, almost casually, triggered, and before the blood-smeared man stumbled and fell to one knee, clutching a raw and bleeding forearm, he had spun the rifle around the trigger-guard, and jacked a fresh shell into the breech.

The downed man howled, nursing his arm across his chest. A second man who had had thoughts about dragging iron, quickly thrust his hands shoulder-high, shaking his head.

'You bunch of miserable hogs!' Quinn said in disgust. 'Judas, come to think of it I wouldn't ask any self-respecting pig to live in that garbage pile you got in there!' There was anger in his voice now. He jerked the rifle. 'On your feet! All of you — yeah, that means you, too, with the wounded arm . . . c'mon, *move*!'

They staggered upright, the wounded man swaying like a sapling in a gale. They stared apprehensively at Quinn.

And rightly so.

'This used to be my home,' he said quietly, raking a bleak gaze over the foursome. 'I lived here, was preparing it for my wife! . . . Now look at what you scum have done to it!'

He jumped the sorrel forward on the last few words and one man screamed as the horse's head smashed him in the face and sent him rolling on the ground, sobbing. Quinn yanked the sorrel's head around quickly and it caught the next man just as he made a desperate leap up, trying to grab Quinn. He floundered in mid-air and Quinn's rifle cracked across his skull and drove him down in a heap. The wounded man started to run away, lurching and zigzagging. Quinn let him go, gave his attention to the other one, a big, bearded ranny with a torn shirt that showed dirt-caked white skin beneath.

He suddenly ducked and shoulder-rolled, coming up with a dead tree branch that had spilled from the nearby wood-pile. He swung it like a club and the sorrel reared up so as to avoid it. The man staggered with his effort and Quinn freed a boot from the stirrup, jumped the horse forward and kicked the man between the shoulders. He flailed and went down to his knees. Quinn leaned from the saddle and clubbed him to the ground with his rifle.

There was no sign of the wounded man and although he could have followed the blood-spot trail easily enough, Quinn let him go.

He was breathing hard, mostly from anger, not exertion. The sick and sorry men he had downed were holding sore heads, groaning.

He walked the horse over to the doorway again, looked inside and tightened his lips. The plans he'd had for this place! Now look at it . . . He wondered how long it had taken them to turn it into the garbage pit it had become.

He dismounted and stepped inside, not very far, his stomach churning at the rancid smell. How any man could stay in this mess for more than a few minutes, let alone *live* here was beyond him . . .

In a savage impulsive movement, he shot out the burning lamp on the table, scattering the rats that were gnawing rotting food. The hot oil sprayed and in moments the rubbish caught and the flames leapt. He stood there grim-faced, watching the flames devour the cabin — the house he had been preparing for Rachel to come to . . .

Now it had been sullied, infected, defiled by Bannister's men. It was better to burn it.

He turned to go back outside and froze.

Four horsemen had come quietly into the yard. Three of them held guns. The fourth man, Marv Daddow, sat easily on his big black, hands folded on his saddle horn.

The injured men were staggering towards the line of riders, coughing in the smoke, one shielding his eyes from the flames that now lit up the clearing.

'Not as neat as you used to have it, Quinn,' Daddow said. 'Likely doin' us all a favour burnin' it down. Mr Bannister aimed to get rid of it sooner or later.' He paused and smiled crookedly. 'Maybe he'll want to thank you for savin' him the trouble.'

'Not necessary.' Quinn held up the rifle and all four riders stiffened. 'What you want me to do with this?'

'Throw it down,' Daddow rasped, eyes narrowed. He looked at the haltered cowpunchers. 'Get out of it. You'd make a billy-goat puke the way you live. They needed that beatin', but that don't change anythin' . . . Best step clear of the fire, Quinn.'

'Change what?' Quinn asked, placing the rifle carefully on the ground as he stepped away from the fire at his back.

'Like this is one of Mr Bannister's line camps now — you abandoned it over three years ago, Quinn. You can't expect to ride in here and take up where you left off.' He paused and added with a crooked smile, 'Leastways, we don't aim to let you.'

Quinn said nothing, wondering just how fast Daddow really was these days. Likely too blamed fast for him. But if he didn't do something, at least make a try at escaping, he knew he was in for the whipping of his life.

Or worse.

Daddow might be a neat and fastidious dresser, but he had a mean streak in him wide as the Mississippi in flood.

'Uh-uh, Quinn, don't be loco — you get froggy and all you'll get is a bullet through the leg or foot. We ain't out to kill you — tonight. Might save that for another time. When I told Mr Bannister you was back he said you'd make for here. 'Teach him a lesson, Marv,' he told me. 'Make him realize things've changed.' And that's just what I aim to do.'

The roof beams had burned through now and the heavy sod collapsed, spewing sparks and fire high into the night. The horses moved restlessly, rolling their eyes as embers showered. Then Daddow jerked his head and Quinn cursed: he had been too busy watching the riders, hadn't paid attention to the men he had beaten after Daddow cussed them out.

It had all been an act. They'd simply scattered, now came on him from two sides, having crept all the way around the burning cabin so as to take him by surprise.

He was faster than he had hoped, getting out his six-gun, and he blasted one man's leg from under him so that when he went down, one of the others tripped over him. He jumped sideways, but they were closing in, eager to take their revenge. Two of the riders had leapt their mounts towards him.

One man leaned out of the saddle,

struck the six-gun from Quinn's grip. He grunted, hugged his numbed wrist to his chest. Rough hands grabbed him, fists battered his ribs, another clipped him on the jaw, and his legs buckled. They held him partly upright and flung him out into the yard.

Marv Daddow had dismounted by now, pulled on a pair of yellow wash-leather work-gloves and motioned for two men to get Quinn on his feet.

Quinn struggled, although only half-conscious, and he got an elbow into one man's mouth and the hardcase stumbled away, spitting a broken tooth and a spoonful of blood.

Fists clubbed him to his knees and fingers twisted in his hair, jerked his head up. Quinn stared up at Daddow and the man swore, flicking at a splash of blood that had soiled his grey shirt.

The glove hit Quinn alongside the head like a smack from a railroad tie. But he couldn't fall away from the pain, because iron hands gripped him, fingers dug into his flesh, and held him in position for Daddow to hit him again — and again . . .

They kept throwing buckets of chill well-water over him whenever he passed out. He could barely see, his eyes were so swollen. He couldn't say enough intelligible words even to cuss them out through his puffed and cut mouth. Air bubbled and spattered through his broken nose. His shirt was ripped almost from his torso and blood shone redly against his white flesh.

A knee occasionally drove into his chest or up under his jaw. Boots thudded the length and breadth of his body. He passed out but always they brought him back.

Daddow could have easily killed him, beaten him to a pulp and left him to die. But he knew his trade well: his blows hurt with maximum pain, but he knew how to pull them so they did no fatal damage. No ribs were splintered. His jaw wasn't broken, he would be able to see again when the swelling went down around his eyes. He might be missing a few teeth but likely he would be able to feed himself later on . . .

He felt the fingers in his hair, heard a voice distantly through the thunderous roaring in his bleeding ears.

'You should've stayed away, Quinn — no one wants you back here. Seein' as you ain't dead like we thought, I guess there might be another reward on your head . . . They'll keep you on the run, some of the scum who come after that five thousand bucks.' Daddow laughed briefly. 'Hell, they'd slit their mother's throat for a tenth of that!'

More water hit him in the face and after a while Daddow spoke again.

'We're turnin' you loose — oh, not around here. Maybe deep in the Wolfpacks, maybe just down at the river at the other end of the valley — whatever, you show some sense and don't never come back. Mr Bannister's bein' generous this time. Me, I'd just as soon put a bullet through your head, but I got my orders.'

Cruel fingers grabbed and twisted his throbbing jaw and he made guttural sounds of pain as Daddow shook him. 'You savvy, Quinn? Just git outta here an' be glad you're still alive. You show even the tip of your nose in these parts again and you'll wake up at the bottom of a canyon I know with a wolf pack fightin' over what's left of you.'

He shook Quinn violently. 'Nod if you savvy!'

Quinn's head rocked on his shoulders with the savage shaking and one of the men said, half laughing,

'Hey, Marv, I b'lieve he nodded!'

'Yeah, think you're right, Crow. Now you're showin' good sense, Quinn. Just drag your ass outta this neck of the woods and send Mr Bannister a 'thank you' telegraph for lettin' you live, an' we'll say no more about anythin'.'

He flung the bloody, barely conscious man to the ground and dipped his aching hands, still in the now torn gloves, into a pail of water. It turned a rust colour as he glanced at the men standing around staring at the battered man on the ground. Two of them began rifling Quinn's pockets.

'Take him as far into the hills as you can and drop him off — don't matter too much whether the fall kills him or not. The wolves'll clean up anythin' that's left — '

5

Wilderness

There was not yet any real light in the sky when he first started to come round, only a faint greyness which promised sun-up soon. At least it gave him a direction and his aching brain suggested they were heading north-east. Which, at that stage, meant little to him.

He was roped to a horse, probably his own sorrel, but he couldn't tell for sure and it hardly mattered.

He could barely see, his eyes were swollen so much. His nose was clotted with thick blood and he was mouth-breathing, throat raspy and sore and dry. His body throbbed and his arms and shoulders throbbed. His legs throbbed — and, most of all, his head — like a balloon had been blown up inside his skull and was trying to burst its way out.

He remembered what had happened but quickly slid over the recollection of the hammering fists and boots, Marv Daddow enjoying every thudding blow. Maybe Daddow wouldn't enjoy the sound of fists hitting flesh if it were his own flesh — and the fists were Quinn's . . .

That day would come. Sometime. He knew that for certain sure, so pushed it away to the back of his thudding brain for now.

The important thing at the moment was how he was going to get out of his present predicament.

There were three men with him. He recognized Crow's voice and he was sure the other two were a couple of the hardcases he had beat up at the cabin before he'd set it afire. OK — he knew *who* was taking him somewhere, but he didn't know where they were or where they were going.

And with his face so battered out of

shape, no more than a slit showing at the corner of his right eye to give him vision, it wasn't likely he was going to find out unless the trio gave it away in conversation.

So he played possum, rocking to the movement of the horse, let his head nod loosely, and listened.

'Just what'd he ever do to Bannister?' a grating voice asked and Crow answered.

'Happened to build on land Bannister wanted.'

The man snorted a laugh. 'Must have a hex on him, pickin' land that Bannister needed to throw up his cabin!'

'I didn't say 'needed', I said 'wanted' — Bannister got this notion of expandin' up the valley to keep it free of sod-busters who were movin' in and smalltimers like Quinn — They crossed swords, Quinn bein' the stubborn sonuva he is, and — well, I won't bother goin' into details, but Bannister and Quinn clashed and after Bannister shot up that cabin, Quinn rustled some of B-Five's stock and ran 'em into a bog.'

'Judas, he plays rough!' This was the third man, a thin, tenor kind of voice.

Crow laughed. 'Rough? Hell, Shack, that Quinn was one of the worst hardnoses Bannister ever seen. One man — and he almost brought Bannister to his knees. Then one day Quinn's not around any more and to make sure he stayed away, Bannister got out a reward dodger on him for the rustlin' . . . '

'Now he's back,' allowed the man with the grating voice.

'Yeah, he's back, all right, Cam. An' you seen what's happened to him — and what's about to happen.'

'Yeah, well how much deeper into these damn hills we gotta go? I'm worried about findin' our way out again.' Shack really sounded anxious and Crow growled in reply.

'Not much further now — we'll find our way out okay. But I wouldn't like to bet on Quinn makin' it — very few white men know these Wolfpack Hills past the falls.'

'Christ, we passed them just after midnight!' Cam said. 'I sure hope you know what you're doin', Crow.'

'Gonna be light soon — we go up to that butte and get rid of him.'

The talk had told Quinn very little. It reminded him of how he'd clashed with Bannister and he remembered it in detail now, but apart from finding out they were in the Wolfpacks, there was little of interest in what the trio had spoken of.

He felt the change in the land, in the up-heaving movement of the horse under him. They seemed to climb for a long time and he could feel the thin warmth of an early sun on his flesh now. But there was still little to see through the small section that allowed him partial sight. Left side, he was blinded completely for now.

The horses were blowing when they finally stopped. One of the men cursed, but in a low voice so that Quinn couldn't tell which one it was.

'What we do now?' That was Shack.

'Over there.'

'Christ, I hope he can fly!'

'I'm here to tell you he can't,' Crow snapped, and Quinn remembered the man never had had much of a sense of humour. 'Get the ropes off him and get him down from the hoss.'

'What'll we do with it?'

'The hoss? Run it over, too.'

'Hell, Crow, that's good hoss-flesh!' protested Cam.

'Take the rifle and saddle-bag first, then do it . . .'

Quinn was dragged roughly from the saddle and he forced himself to stay limp while they untied him. He heard the sorrel snort and stomp and he started to lift his head just as it shrilled wildly. There was a crumbling sound, a pattering of falling rocks and the fading whinny of the horse going off what Quinn figured to be a high ledge. He heard the heavy carcase strike, the sounds of a slide, and finally *silence*.

'Damn! I hated to do that!' Cam said.

'Now Quinn . . . ' Crow ordered flatly.

Shack was holding lightly to Quinn's left arm and he knew if once Cam grabbed his right, he wouldn't have any chance of controlling things. As it was he was on his knees and Shack started to drag him upright.

Working almost totally blind, Quinn swung into the man, hooked him in the belly. Shack was taken by surprise, gagged, loosened his grip, and Quinn spun back, arms flailing. He was lucky. One fist hit the approaching Cam smack in the face and the man yelled in pain as he stumbled, sat down with a thud. Crow cursed and started to dismount, but Shack still held the knife he had used to cut Quinn's bonds and he lunged forward, struck downwards with the blade.

Quinn didn't even see it coming, felt

the searing pain as the steel sliced deep into his left upper arm. Pure instinct guided his knee into Shack's crotch and the man screamed, retched, sprawled dangerously close to the edge. There was a blur rushing towards Quinn as he started to pull the knife out of his arm.

He stepped back swiftly — and next thing he was falling through space, hearing above the rush of the air past his ears, the mocking laughter of Crow above.

'Happy landings, Quinn!'

He smashed into some bushes which were springy enough to absorb some of the shock and to hurl him outwards so that he continued to fall. Next time he struck earth and he tumbled out of control, sliding and skidding until once more he shot out into space and after a brief sensation of falling, splashed into icy water and plunged deep into green, enfolding depths . . . down . . . down . . .

* * *

Bannister was a neat-looking man of about five feet eight, slim build, and with a cap of black hair plastered flat across his bullet skull. His face was pleasant enough, if you discounted the chill look that frosted over his grey eyes now as he looked at Crow standing awkwardly on the floor rug in front of his boss's desk.

'He never surfaced?' Bannister asked in a deceptively quiet voice and Crow winced, recognising this sign that the rancher was not pleased.

'Well — we seen somethin' goin' down the rapids a couple minutes later, Mr Bannister.' The rancher did not like to be called 'boss' by his men, and insisted that all his employees call him 'Mister'. 'The pool emptied down a slope and became rapids and it likely was him.'

Bannister's slim fingers tapped a tattoo on the edge of his desk, another signal that his mood was deteriorating rapidly. He flicked his gaze across to the corner where Marv Daddow stood against a wall, arms folded, face impassive.

'What exactly were your orders, Marv?'

Daddow cleared his throat. 'I said take Quinn deep into the Wolfpacks, dump him and never mind how — that the wolves'd clean up in the end.'

He straightened suddenly as Bannister's fist smashed down onto the desk. 'You fool! I said teach him a lesson! Not kill him!'

Daddow's eyes widened a little now and Crow breathed a mite easier now that Bannister's anger had been turned onto the gunman. 'I just figured he likely wouldn't make it outta the hills, Mr Bannister — I — I never gave no orders for him to be killed outright.'

Bannister didn't shift his gaze at Daddow's attempt to divert his rage back to Crow. He spoke bitterly.

'Dump him in the worst wilderness in this territory and let the wolves clean up after you, and that's not ordering the man's death?'

Daddow moved a mite uncomfortably, but his gaze didn't waver, either. He knew he would take only so much from Bannister — or any man — and then he would settle things with his gun. Bannister knew it, too, and it always puzzled Daddow that the man never seemed fazed by the possibility that his hired gun might suddenly turn on him.

A fearless son of a bitch — or just so arrogant and used to getting his own way that he couldn't conceive of anything stopping him from getting what he wanted . . .

'Listen, Mr Bannister, I beat him to within an inch of his life. He was alive when Crow and the others rode him out . . . What they did up there in the hills has nothin' to do with me. I carried out my part.'

'To your satisfaction, maybe,' Bannister said, and turned to Crow. 'You think there's a chance he might still be alive? C'mon, man! I want the truth! You'll come to more harm hedging it than by telling me what you really think . . . '

Crow moved from one foot to the other. 'We-ell — he's one tough bastard, Mister Bannister — if he could survive them rapids, with Shack's knife in him, he just might make it ashore somewhere downstream. That's if he even survived the fall.'

'And you never stayed around to find out!'

'It was a long ride out, Mister Bannister! Took us till near sundown to get clear of them Wolfpacks . . . '

His voice trailed off as Bannister scowled and looked back to Daddow. 'Marv, I'm putting this on your shoulders, holding you responsible. Take some men and go back in there and find Quinn. Bring me his body if you find him dead — '

'And drag him back at the end of a rope if he's still alive?'

Bannister frowned thoughtfully. 'Not necessarily . . . there just might be some profit in — following him.'

Daddow actually blinked. 'I don't get

it, Mister Bannister . . .'

'No — of course you wouldn't. Crow, you go and start organizing some supplies and horses for a trek into the Wolfpacks while I explain a few things to Marv . . . And take the men you had with you earlier. They messed things up, so it's only fair they — and you — set them right.'

Crow nodded, ran a tongue around his lips and hurried out, still bewildered, but cussing at the thought of having to drag-ass all the way back into the goddamn Wolfpack ranges again.

The 'wolf' in the name wasn't there just to pretty things up. It meant exactly what it said — the place was full of prowling packs of wolves and any man, on horse or afoot, would be lucky if he wasn't torn to pieces within hours.

He hoped they would find Quinn's few bloody remains quickly so they could get the hell out.

* * *

As a boy, he had learned early how to ride the rapids, for the Black Hills had many wild streams that tumbled down the hidden canyons and the semi-sacred, secret world of the Lakota Sioux.

If the rapids were shallow, go down feet first, on your back, using your hands like fins or rudders to guide you around obstacles. If they were deep and tumbling, roll onto your belly, head-first, snatching breaths of air in the hollows between waves, watching for eddies and swirls that you could use to work your way in to the bank . . .

It was no fun going down this latter way with a knife sticking out of his upper arm, but the white-water was wild and roaring and he had been spewed out of that deep green pool like a cork firing from a shaken soda-pop bottle. Luckily, he'd landed on his belly and he rode the foaming green-and-brown flood, snatching his head up, trying to see where he was going. The icy water had reduced the swelling some almost instantly and he could see better, but far from clearly.

Everything seemed to be viewed through a screen of cheesecloth and he couldn't judge distance. As if he didn't have enough bruises, he collected a couple of dozen more from sunken rocks and jammed logs he didn't see until too late. But his body told him how the currents were in between the violent white-water surges, and by the time he was three miles downstream, he had managed to get into water shallow enough to stand in.

His legs were like jelly, wobbling and giving way, but he floundered ashore and dragged himself under a rock overhang where he lay on his back, gasping, chest heaving mightily. When his breathing had settled some, he found a piece of driftwood, jammed it between his aching jaws and bit down on it as he grasped the heft of the knife and pulled it out of his arm.

He yelled involuntarily with the pain, felt the welling of fresh blood, tore a strip off his ruined shirt and wrapped it around his arm, using his teeth to draw a knot tight over the wound.

He was exhausted by then and edged back as far as he could beneath the rock. He knew he would never hear anyone who came to search for him: he was too close to the roaring water for that.

He groped and found the knife, looked at it but could only make out that it was nothing unusual, just a stag-handled hunting knife like many cowboys carried.

But he had a weapon. And he knew from past experience that a knife was all a man needed to survive in the wilderness, as long as he kept his head and didn't panic when food and water were short.

He almost laughed. At least he didn't have to worry about water!

It struck him as hilariously funny then and his battered body shuddered as the laughter gripped him — but only briefly.

It faded quickly as he slipped away into unconsciousness.

* * *

Although he tossed and turned, shivering, he didn't fully awaken until there was a grey light streaking the east. He immediately felt the pain that coursed throughout his throbbing body — and the sense of tightness and increase in size of his left arm.

Exploring fingers found the swollen flesh bulging over the narrow bandage he had wrapped around — how long ago? He carefully cut the too-tight strip of cloth away and gritted his teeth as pain almost knocked him out as it swept through the swollen, inflamed wound. When he had his breath back he found he could see more clearly, though his eyes were gritty and paining him. He realised with a shock that another day was coming, which meant he'd slept for almost twenty-four hours.

The world was an unsteady place for him and he fell several times, even though he was moving on hands and knees, before he reached the edge of the river. He plunged his hot face into the chill water, wrenched his head up, gasping, then scooped handfuls of water up to his mouth. He swallowed slowly for his throat ached, and a shiver ran through him.

Quinn recognized it for what it was: the first signs that he was running a fever, due to spreading infection in his arm wound . . .

God knew what a man like Shack might have left on the knife blade! He wasn't a man who'd keep his knife cleaned.

He would have to go into the woods now, seek out special herbs and healing bark if he was to fight the infection. If he didn't do it successfully, he could die . . .

But he had no sooner had the thought than something made him glance upstream and across the river. There was movement in the brush there and even as he edged back beneath his rock slab he saw the horsemen.

Three of them. No, four, the other man showing ten yards further downstream. For a wild moment Quinn thought he had been seen, but the fourth man, Marv Daddow, called to the others.

'Reckon his body wouldn't've come down this far. Too many little coves and shallows between them rapids and here — he'd've washed-up back the way we've just come.'

Crow snorted. 'Well, we looked good and we din' find hide nor hair of him . . . I reckon he wouldn't be alive anyway this far down. He'd of drowned for sure.'

Cam and Shack agreed and Daddow rode up to them, answering curtly. 'Then find his body to take back to Mister Bannister! He wants to see it.'

The trio said nothing and by that time the roaring of the river drowned out any conversation the men were having with Daddow.

Quinn crouched, his senses spinning, unconsciously gripping the knife hard in his right hand. His left arm hung uselessly, standing a little way out from his side because of the swelling. He tried to jam himself as far back as possible under the overhang of rock, his head feeling as if it would explode. Then the men split up, two crossing the river in a shallow part so they could mount a search on both banks.

Quinn was shivering badly now, his vision blurred, his mind spinning as he fought to keep out delirious thoughts as the infection fevered his battered body.

Quinn heard the muted drone of their voices as they searched but couldn't make out any words. Shack and Crow worked this side but desultorily, as if their hearts weren't in it. He figured they believed he had drowned and his body was jammed under a rock somewhere upstream, or a long way from here, anyway. If they thought to look under this overhang, he knew he was a dead man. He was too weak to fight and, anyway, he figured they wouldn't give him a chance. He'd be a sitting duck and they'd just empty a gun into him and then drag out what was left and leave it for the wolves . . .

Across the river, Crow and Daddow rode slowly, poking at piles of debris with sapling poles, looking behind deadfalls and logs that had been washed up by the waters.

Twice Daddow retraced his steps, then put his mount over to Quinn's side of the river and searched again where Crow and Shack had ridden. He actually leaned from the saddle a little and poked under the very rock where Quinn crouched in such agony. The sapling end slid between Quinn's knees and the rock, dragged across one of his bent legs and scraped across the coarse wet sand before it was withdrawn.

Daddow, muttering briefly, moved on, swearing . . .

Quinn reckoned it was more than an

hour later when he crawled out to take a look. He must have passed out just after they had gone by, he figured, for the sun was higher, reflected blindingly from the roaring river.

His eyes were still sunken behind bruised, puffy flesh, but he could see reasonably well — and there wasn't a rider anywhere in sight . . .

It looked safe, but he stayed put for another hour before finally venturing out. He was close to passing out again, so he crawled into some grass, arranged it around him to hide his body, and lay there in the sun's warmth. It eased the shaking some. The wound looked ugly but the sun's warmth felt good against the swollen flesh.

He was on the verge of delirium and he had to fight to hold control. There was no choice: he had to find the plants he needed before he keeled over again, or he was going to drift into a coma and likely never wake up.

And in the background, all the time, was the knowledge that killers were relentlessly hunting him . . .

He crawled to some willows, scraped some outer bark, then cut through the protective layer and hacked out a square of the soft inner bark. He rolled his scrapings in this and breathing hard, sat back to recover before moving on.

He found thyme, which he chewed as he went along, for it was a known antiseptic and had the advantage of reducing a man's body odour if he ate enough. If Daddow brought in dogs to track him, this would be an advantage.

There were plenty of dandelions but they didn't taste so good in the raw, but there was some nourishment and they were good for digestion: God alone knew what he might have to eat in order to survive so a little prevention wouldn't go astray. He pounded parts of a plantain plant to make a compress for his wound.

By the time he found some birch trees, he couldn't go any further and he rested quite a while before summoning enough energy to cut some oblongs out of the bark. It was mighty awkward because his left hand was almost useless, the fingers swollen and splayed, barely able to bend. But he scraped the soft inner bark away and carefully folded the rest into a crude dish-shaped container. He pinned the folds near the top with split twigs and half-filled it with water.

Fire was his big problem. Making it was one thing — and none too easy at that, half-crippled as he was — but the chance it might give him away was another. And all too real . . .

He knew he didn't have the strength or dexterity to make fire without matches unless he could find some flint. He sprinkled his collected willow bark on top of the water: it could be cold-extracting while he tackled this next problem.

He forced himself to crawl around, examining any stone he came across, and finally he found one that gave a good, hot-yellow shower of sparks when he struck its edge with the back of the knife blade.

Tinder was the next step and he shredded dry grass, gathered a handful of pine needles, pounding them into a resinous pulp. His clothes had dried out on him by now and he turned his pockets inside out, scraped out the lint that had gathered there, and also in the seams. This was excellent for tinder.

He dragged his meagre gear behind a mound of earth, cut out a square of grass and dug a shallow trench with the knife blade, all beneath the low-hanging branch of a young pine: it would help disperse any smoke.

In five minutes his tinder smouldered, burst into flame as he blew on it gently, and minutes later he had a hot, almost smokeless fire burning. He fed it dry twigs and allowed them to burn down to a bed of embers. He set the birch-bark container crosswise above them, heating the willow bark solution also dropping in hot stones. This would break his fever!

The thought boosted his morale — then the wolf packs started to howl. They seemed to be all around him.

6

Dangerous Game

Daddow, his clothes torn and dirty, sweat-dark in patches, reined his mount down on the edge of a ravine. He pushed his hat to the back of his head and used his shirt sleeve to blot sweat from his stubbled face. He wrinkled his nose as he caught a whiff of his body odour and he swore, spat, took out a cheroot and lit up.

Far below, he saw Cam and Shack wading their horses across the meandering stream and he waved his hat, caught Shack's eye. He signalled impatiently for them to hurry to the rendezvous, and looked around him sourly. Crow rode out of the trees and set his weary horse across the broken rock to where Marv Daddow waited.

'You're late!' Daddow snapped.

Crow shrugged. 'You ain't been here long — seen you climbin' that ridge when I was halfway up. Called out but you never heard me.'

Daddow grunted. He stood in the stirrups and shaded his eyes as he looked all around the savage, wild country spread out below. He bared his teeth and shook his head.

'Where the hell *is* the son of a bitch, Crow! He's gotta be down there somewhere . . . We know he's alive, findin' that fire and the trees with the squares cut out of them proves that — But *where in hell has he gone?*'

Crow shrugged, rolling a cigarette from a slim tobacco sack. 'If he's still alive . . . '

'Of course he is, you damn fool! He's alive and laughin' at us!'

'OK — but he's hidin' his tracks damn well. Can't be hurt that bad.'

Daddow looked savage, glaring at Crow as if it was his fault. 'He may be hurt enough to hole-up somewhere.

That's why we ain't findin' any fresh tracks.'

Crow lit his cigarette. 'Could be, I'll allow that — but we done searched under almost every goddamn bush an' rock between the falls and this ravine. I'd like to know where the bastard's holed-up — if he is.'

Daddow was about to vent some of his spleen in a savage retort but by then Shack and Cam were coming out of the timber. He knew by their hang-dog looks that they had had no success. But Shack, surprisingly, made a good suggestion.

'Marv, me an' Cam been thinkin' . . . He's either holed-up in some place good, or he's not hurt bad an' he's managin' to cover his tracks mighty good.'

'Take you three goddamn days to figure that?' Daddow snapped.

'No, but — well, we ain't gettin' anywheres, and you don't seem inclined to quit . . . '

'There'll be no quittin'! Mister

Bannister wants proof either way that Quinn's still alive — or dead. Now we give him that proof if it takes us six months! You all savvy that?'

They mumbled or grumbled in assent and Shack, looking a mite leery, said quietly, 'Well, whatever's happened to Quinn he's out-foxed us somehow. We're all pretty good trackers but we don't seem good enough for this chore — we need help.'

'I'll go along with that,' Cam grated, working his stiff shoulders. 'I'm plumb tuckered from tryin' to pick up his trail.'

'Yeah, what we need is an Injun, Marv,' said Shack and suddenly straightened in his saddle as he saw the way Daddow looked at him — sharply, eyes narrowed, his face rock-hard.

'What'd you say?' Marv Daddow asked quietly and Shack squirmed, wishing he'd kept his mouth shut.

'Aw, I'm just tuckered out, too, Marv — I was just jawin' . . . '

'What — did — you — *say*?'

Shack swallowed. 'I said we — we need an Injun to help us . . . but I . . .'

He bit off the rest as Daddow nodded several times. 'Yeah, you're right — should've figured it before. Quinn's half-Sioux or Cheyenne or somethin' — we under-estimated him. Never thought about his Injun side . . . '

'Hell, I wouldn't go approachin' none of the Injuns that run in these hills, Marv!' Crow said. 'Half of 'em've never stopped hatin' the white man.'

'*Every* Injun still hates the white-eyes, you blamed fool! They just pretend they don't so's we'll give 'em grub an' blankets and so on — but I know where we can find one who'll help. Christ, I can't believe I never thought of it before! Judas, you wait here and I'll be back sometime tomorrow . . . And by the day after, we'll have Travis Quinn's scalp!'

* * *

Claire knew it was too soon — ask her *how* she knew and she wouldn't be able to say, but some inner sense told her that it would be some time yet before Dave Callahan's dust appeared in the high pass over Patterson's Peak. If it ever did . . .

Still, carrying Donny astride her hip, she walked first into the hot sun of the yard, shading her eyes with her free hand. Then, when she couldn't see the section of pass she wanted to her satisfaction, she hitched up the boy, slid him around to her back and, giggling, he put his two small arms around her neck.

'And a-way we go-*oooooo*!' she cried and moved off at a lumbering 'gallop', every few steps imitating a horse arching its back preparatory to a buck-jump. Donny laughed aloud, ecstatic face flushed with excitement.

Claire was breathless by the time she reached the top of the hogback rise behind the corrals and she let the boy slide down to the ground where he started chasing a lizard while she looked again up to the high pass.

Still no dust. She allowed Donny to play for half an hour, watching the pass every so often.

Then she took his dusty hand and together they walked back towards the house.

'Daddy no . . . ?' the child asked, startling her and she forced a smile, tousled his hair.

'Not today, darling — but soon.'

'Yes — soon.'

Her teeth tugged at her bottom lip and her hand squeezed the boy's as a single tear slid down her face.

'Oh, Davey!' she breathed.

Like a fervent prayer.

* * *

Quinn found the cave by accident.

He was awkwardly cutting a sapling to make into a spear, for both protection and hunting protein in the form of meat, when he saw a small animal scampering up the slope. It disappeared swiftly into what he thought was the shadow of an overhang of rock but when it didn't come out again, he climbed up out of curiosity. It had likely been a ground squirrel but there was no sign of it in the small cave he discovered although the place smelled strongly enough of animal.

It sloped back sharply from the opening but was partly screened by brush and there were loose rocks nearby he knew he could use to make a wall for shielding a fire. It was cool inside, and later he was to find out it was like a freezing chamber at night but he dragged himself in, along with the embryonic spear and his charred and battered, though still useable, birchbark pot.

His left arm was all but useless, even though it felt some better when he put on the poultices of plantain and moss. But there was still a lot of pus oozing and he had tried draining it by using strips of cloth cut from the remains of his shirt, changing them frequently, without much success . . . The fever was working in him, with him all day and night — *worse* at night — but so far he had kept it to a manageable level. Using his good arm, he built his small wall of rocks at an angle near the cave entrance, used his knife to scoop out a hole towards the rear of the cave. He would build his fire here. Then he put two flat rocks between it and the entrance as an added screen and so they would also reflect the heat onto the bed of pine boughs he made for himself.

The work exhausted him, but in late afternoon, he made one more trip and brought back arm-loads of grass. Some he used on his bed. The rest he made into cord, rolling it across his thigh wearily. It would be considered a disgrace by even the youngest Lakota child but it would have to do.

Near sundown, he crawled outside and rigged his animal trap, placing it across a barely distinguishable pad, propping the noose open with a twig, fixing the cord to a springy sapling. After dark he heard the dying screams of a strangling animal but was too weak to crawl outside to see what he had caught.

He had a night of delirium but, come morning, found a jack-rabbit hanging from the springy sapling he had used to whip the noose and its catch high, snapping the neck swiftly.

He skinned it badly because of his swollen left hand, hacked up the corpse and made a stew, flavouring it with wild onion, sage, marjoram and thyme. He felt better after he had eaten, and wondered how much longer his birchbark pot would serve him. The more it dried, the more it charred and it wouldn't be long before a hole was burned through.

He forced himself to work on his spear, chopping a crude point then rubbing it smooth and sharp on the rocks before hardening it in the embers of his fire.

Although he had heard the wolf packs howling each night, he had only sighted two *lobos*, and they had been in the distance. But they would pick up his scent sooner or later and he needed some sort of weapon. A bow and arrow would be good but he was not up to making such a weapon at the moment. Maybe later . . .

For now he was reasonably content: he had some of the stew left, some edible plants, and had found a small spring trickling down at the rear of the cave. It took an hour to fill the cone-shaped birchbark cup he had made, but it was pure, cool water . . .

But rest was important for his recovery — not to mention better food. Which meant protein — meat — which, in turn, meant he would have to go a'hunting. But — later . . .

He curled up stiffly on his bed of boughs, daunted by the prospect.

* * *

The Indian was part Comanche, part Cheyenne, and went by the name of Firebird. But white men called him 'Bird'. He had spent many years scouting and tracking for the cavalry but now worked as a roustabout at the trading post along the Catamount trail.

He wore his iron-grey hair in braids, with various leather and bone totems worked through them and usually a red-tipped eagle's feather dangled from a beaded clip at the back of his head. His eye colour matched his hair and his nose was hooked, his skin wrinkled leather. No one, including Bird himself, knew his exact age, but most men put him in his sixties.

He was mighty spry for a man of those years and had a liking for the white man's chewing tobacco.

Marv Daddow promised him twenty dollars and a two-pound pack of *Ozark Chaw* if he would come with him back to the Wolfpacks.

'Want you to track a wounded white man,' Daddow told him in the dimness of the smelly trading room of the post, amongst the stacks of animal hides, bags of flour and rotting vegetables that the trader would foist upon reservation-skipping bucks when he had the chance. He was called Smoke, and had been pickling his liver for years with the rot-gut fire-water he brewed up in his own still, in the root cellar beneath the floor of the post. He had one eye, the empty socket sometimes weeping, and a mouthful of broken teeth.

Now he squinted his good eye at Daddow and said, 'Gonna cost you fifty bucks to take my man away from his work. He goes, it means *I* gotta ride all the way to Catamount for goods.'

Daddow glared. 'I'll get to you later — first-off, I want to know if Bird's comin'.'

'He only goes if I say so!' growled Smoke, sipping cloudy liquid from a grimy jelly jar.

Daddow ignored him, looking at the Indian. 'Well, chief? What you say?'

Bird nodded. 'I get horse.'

As he started out Smoke reached under the counter and laid a dusty sawed-off shotgun next to his jar.

'Daddow, I need to see that fifty bucks before Bird even saddles-up.' The Indian closed the door quietly behind him.

Daddow threw him a hard look. 'I'll give you ten.'

'You'll gimme fifty or you ride out alone — if you ride out at all.' He grinned, showing his smashed teeth like mossy tombstones in a neglected cemetery, and laid a hand casually on the shotgun. He arched his eyebrows quizzically. 'That's the deal.'

Daddow's face didn't change and after a long minute, he shrugged and sighed. 'OK — it's your place and he's your Injun, I guess. But he better be as good as I've heard.'

Smoke relaxed some now although he kept his hand on the shotgun. His grin widened. 'Bird's good, all right — if you catch him just right. Moody kinda sonuva, though. Er — you wanna gimme that fifty now?'

'Sure . . . dunno just how much I've got in here . . . '

Daddow dug a hand into his trouser pocket and flung a handful of silver and gold coins onto the counter. Smoke's hungry eye lit-up and he instinctively lunged with both hands to prevent any falling to the floor.

In an instant, Daddow stepped forward, grabbed the startled trader by the ears and smashed his face into the hardwood counter. The nose went audibly and blood sprayed. Daddow flung the dazed, bloody-faced trader back against the wall, vaulted the counter, drove both feet into the man's chest. Smoke grunted and his knees folded.

Daddow twisted fingers into the collar of the filthy shirt, dragged the man across to the trapdoor leading down into the cellar where the liquor still bubbled constantly. He flung Smoke down unceremoniously and the trader sprawled, barely conscious, groaning.

Daddow, breathing a little fast, took out a cheroot from his vest pocket and lit it. He dragged deeply until it had a fine, burning ash, went down the slippery steps and looked across at the copper still.

The heat hit him solidly and his eyes stung with the fumes. He kicked over the metal pail beneath the cooling-coil where a trickle of foul-looking liquor spilled into the half-full vessel.

Rot-gut flooded the cellar and Daddow knelt, drew deeply on his cheroot again, the ash going past the half-way mark this time, and buried the butt so that the ash was just above the surface of a pool of liquid.

On the way to the steps, he kicked Smoke viciously. 'You bastard! The likes of you don't never get the best of Marv Daddow! Go to hell now, like a good feller!'

Chuckling, he hurried up, closed the trap and left the store, taking the box of

Ozark Chaw tobacco with him.

Outside, Bird was walking slowly up from the corrals leading a long-in-the-tooth Appaloosa mount, and a second horse, a chestnut, carrying a couple of empty-looking panniers. Daddow called out, 'Mount up and let's go, Bird!'

The Indian gave him a brief, strange look, and Daddow thought he could almost hear the bones creak as the old man climbed into the saddle. Yet he did it fluidly enough.

They were almost to the line of trees when there was a *whoosh*! behind them and both hipped in their saddles.

Flames were licking out of the windows and door of the trading post. The Indian snapped his head around on his turkey neck, braids swinging, iron-grey eyes fixing on Daddow's face.

'Where there's Smoke, there's fire, huh?' the gunman said with a crooked grin and then both men threw arms across their eyes as the trading post exploded, splintered wood buzzing through the hot, insect-laden air of the afternoon. A heat blast hit them as they fought their prancing horses.

When the mounts were still and the ruins of the post burned away, several small fires starting from blazing debris, Daddow said, 'Learn a lesson from that, Bird — no one tries to put anythin' over on Marv Daddow. Know what I mean?'

Bird said nothing, turned his two horses and rode on towards the hills. Smiling crookedly, Daddow followed.

Shortly he began to whistle.

* * *

Daddow and Bird met Crow and the others at the pre-arranged rendezvous around mid-morning.

'You sure he's still alive, Marv?' asked Cam, considering himself to be the comedian of the group.

'Ask him,' growled Daddow, watering his horse and splashing water over his hot face.

Cam winked at Shack. 'You still alive, Bird? Or you just a ghost taggin' along for a little chawin' baccy?'

'Not ghost yet — but when I am, might come back and haunt you, Cam.'

The others laughed and Cam scowled. 'Smart-ass old Injun! Go on, git downwind of me! You stink!'

Bird wrinkled his large nose. 'You sure it me?' But he moved his horses downwind and Crow asked Daddow, 'Where'll we start, Marv? He don't look like he could find his own pecker.'

'You find young squaw, I find pecker,' Bird assured them and even Cam grinned.

'He's good. I used him once before when Mr Bannister wanted a feller bad . . . Come here, Bird.'

Daddow led the way into the brush and pointed to the birch tree with the squares of bark removed, walked across and showed him the oblong of dead grass where Quinn had built his fire. Bird squatted, grunting, studying the ground for a long time.

'Hey, he gone to sleep?' asked Cam,

needling, pushing Bird's shoulder roughly.

The old Indian almost over-balanced, turned his head slowly, let his gaze settle on Daddow.

'Tracks old.'

'Yeah — few days. But you can pick up more can't you?'

'Know these tracks.'

'What? What you mean 'know' 'em?'

'See this man before — Quinn.'

The white men exchanged glances. Daddow nodded slowly. 'Ye-ah — it's Travis Quinn . . . That bother you?'

'Dangerous man.'

'So he thinks — but you just track him down. We'll worry about how dangerous Quinn is once we catch up with him.'

'How long since you seen Quinn's tracks?' asked Shack suddenly, suspiciously. 'Before these here, I mean.'

'Many moons.'

'Quit that Injun talk! I asked how *long*, dammit!'

'White man year . . . ' Bird fumbled with his own wrinkled, knobbly fingers and looked up again, smiling toothlessly. 'Mebbe t'ree . . . if I count right. I only old Injun.'

Crow spat. 'An' you say you can recognize 'em? After all that time? Hogwash! Someone told you it was Quinn!'

Daddow said quietly as they scoffed at Bird, 'I never told him it was Quinn we were trailin'.'

That stopped them — and by then they realized Bird was mounted and moving away into the woods, leading the chestnut.

'He *can't* be that good!' growled Crow.

Daddow shrugged, settled down on a rock and lit a cheroot. 'We'll see . . . Let him go a spell and see how far along he gets. If he picks up tracks we missed, we'll know he's as good as they say . . . Hey, Bird! We'll sit this one out!'

The others were ready enough to keep lounging about in the shade of the trees and Daddow called after the Indian, 'You come back and report before sundown, Bird — if you got somethin' really good, fire a coupla shots with that old rifle you got on your saddle.'

'If it don't blow up in his face!' Cam grated, chuckling.

Bird gave no sign that he had heard, checked out some more tracks and went deeper into the woods . . .

Come sundown, he hadn't returned, and they hadn't heard any gunshots. The white men began to worry.

When he hadn't come back by daylight, they knew he wasn't going to return at all.

* * *

Quinn was losing his battle with the fever.

The poultices weren't good enough to fight the infection. His arm was swollen almost as large as his thigh, purple and red, throbbing painfully. Pus and watery-looking blood oozed from the lower end of the cut and the flesh was hot to the touch.

Delirium rode him and he spent a night of wild dreams, one of which was to stay with him for a long time . . .

He was chasing a yellow-haired woman and a child who held tightly to her hand. There was a storm and suddenly the earth gave way beneath them and he lunged for the broken edge, reaching for the yellow-haired woman's clutching hand.

Then he was jerked back violently and he rolled onto his back, saw a wild-eyed, black-haired woman, naked body gleaming in the rain, tugging at his arm, pulling him away from the edge. He heard the yellow-haired woman's fading scream as she fell into the pit. The child, apparently, didn't make any sound . . .

He awoke drenched in sweat, shouting, making growling noises in his throat. His eyes burned as they stood out of their sockets. His arm seared from shoulder to fingertips.

Breath came laboriously, painfully, and he rolled onto his right side, realising the growling sounds were still going on — yet he wasn't making them.

Quinn shuddered, stiffened as he saw the red eyes gleaming in the darkness. At first he thought it was still part of the nightmare, but he *knew* he was wide awake now — weak and shaken and disoriented, but *awake*!

Then he glimpsed the shape behind the eyes, against the faint grey of the cave mouth.

It was a wolf.

Coming for him . . .

And it wasn't alone.

7

Run From the Pack

He was too weak throw the heavy spear. It was all he could manage to grasp the end of it where it lay beside his bed of boughs and drag it slowly up so he could get some kind of firm grip on it.

The left hand was useless but he held the spear just above the middle with his right as tightly as he could. There was an awkward — and painful — moment when he somehow managed to work the rear of the shaft under his swollen left arm and dig the butt into the wall behind him.

By then he was reeling with exhaustion, his vision blurred by sweat and pain and fever, but he hadn't taken his aching eyes off the dark, indistinct shape of the wolf during the whole process of getting the spear into position.

The animal acted typically, snarling, slavering, driven by hunger — but moving towards him only an inch at a time. It was crouched low, belly almost dragging on the cave floor, leg muscles ready to spring wildly — into flight if danger threatened.

Quinn shook his head in an effort to clear it. The spear moved aside, off the line of the wolf. And the animal took its chance, leaping towards him, fangs bared and dripping saliva.

Rabies flashed into his mind and he almost laughed. Christ, here he was about to be eaten alive and he was worrying about getting *rabies* from a single bite!

He came back to reality with a jolt, and swung the point of the spear into line as the wolf descended for the kill.

There was a smashing impact, a blood-chilling howl, a terrific weight bearing him back and down, crushing him against the wall. Hot saliva splashed into his face.

He felt the wolf's blood running over his right hand where he gripped the spear, unaware that he was screaming and shouting insanely, hoping the noise would deter his attacker.

But the spear had driven home, impaled the wolf, going up through the chest cavity, destroying the heart and lungs, emerging almost between the shoulders.

The wiry, smelly body twisted frantically in death throes and the spear snapped, was wrenched from Quinn's hand. His side was torn by the splintered shaft and his bad arm flooded with pain. Bright lights exploded behind his eyes and his head felt as if it had been split by a tomahawk.

The wolf fell across his legs, thrashed off, the bloody haft of the broken spear whipping about dangerously. It jumped high enough to hit the low cave roof, fell on its side, kicking feebly, tongue lolling, the snarling sounds dying as its body slowly stilled.

Then he heard the others coming.

He wiped stinging sweat from his eyes, made out at least three — no, *four* — forms hunching low as they came belly-down across the floor. Maybe they would feed on the dead wolf, he thought, but while two sniffed at their impaled companion, the other two came on, spreading out so that he had to move his head to keep both in the ambit of his vision.

Quinn knew this was it. The end. Thirty-some years and it had been a hard but fair-enough life for a man who had lived the way he had. He wished he could have settled this thing, though — the 'Dave Callahan'/Travis Quinn business. He thought of Claire — the yellow-haired woman of his nightmares — and the child. *And* the dark-haired, wild-eyed woman . . .

Well, he'd never know how it all fitted together now.

He fumbled up his knife: at least he'd gut one of the devils before the fangs tore his throat out . . .

Then the cave seemed to explode.

Crashing detonations assaulted his ears. Flame stabbed from the direction of the entrance. He heard a bullet whine and snarl in ricochet, and instinctively threw himself flat. The wolves howled and leapt in agony, yelped in terror, as the hail of lead cut them down one by one — and swiftly!

Ears ringing, head spinning, he blinked and coughed in the rasping gunsmoke, and glimpsed a figure coming through the thick blue haze towards him, a rifle dangling from one hand.

Then the hot muzzle with the wisp of smoke curling from it prodded him in the chest and a foot pinned his hand to the rocky floor, making him release his hold on the knife.

At about that point, he passed out, dropping away into another world that was as cold and black as death itself.

* * *

Shack was grumbling, building the cooking fire in the chill of early morning, while the others were greeting the day in their own way.

Marv Daddow urinated against an elm tree, swaying slightly on his feet, eyes half-closed. Cam tried to pull the hole in his left sock around so that his big toe didn't keep popping out inside his boot. Crow was hawking down on one knee, at the same time trying to roll a cigarette, the first of many for the day.

Then Shack froze, poking kindling into the embryo fire. He looked up at the brightening sky through the leaves above his head.

'You hear that?' he asked but only Daddow showed enough interest to turn his head as he buttoned-up his trouser front.

'What?' he asked and there was a growling annoyance in the single word. He had been on edge and in a lousy mood since the Indian had walked out on them and they had had trouble finding his tracks.

'Sounded like gunshots,' Shack said, and that got the others' attention. 'Far-off, kinda dull — mebbe six or seven.'

Daddow spat. 'You're hearin' things.' He glared at the others. 'You two hear 'em?'

Cam shook his head instantly but Crow hesitated. 'Well?' snapped Daddow impatiently.

'Dunno, Marv. My ears were kinda ringin' from all the coughin' but — seems I did hear a kinda — dyin' echo. Coulda been gunfire.'

Daddow frowned. Crow could be a mean, irritating son of a bitch at times, but on a manhunt he was usually on the ball and if *he* backed Shack then maybe there was something in it.

'Where'd they come from?' Marv Daddow asked more reasonably. 'No! Don't look at each other! Turn your backs and just point!'

Shack and Crow obeyed, lifting their right arms — both in the direction of a distant ridge.

Daddow pursed his lips. Cam continued to fight his losing battle with the hole in his sock.

'We got no real tracks to follow,' Daddow decided. 'We'll eat first, then head for that ridge and scout around.'

'Reckon it was Bird's signal, callin' us in?' asked Cam and Daddow scowled.

'After two days? What you use for brains? He's gone, skipped with my money and the tobacco — I'll fix the sonuva sometime . . . He knows I will. He wouldn't be callin' us to him.'

'Then what was the shootin' all about?'

'I guess we'll just have to wait and see, won't we?' snapped Daddow. 'C'mon, Shack, get that goddamn fire goin' — I'm hungry. And I want to check out that ridge . . . '

His bad mood had returned with a vengeance. Not only was he seething at the way the old Indian had simply ridden off and left not even enough tracks for them to be certain which way he'd gone, but this was more time taken up in the search now.

Daddow had always prided himself on his ability to deliver, had built a reputation for it. But this time . . . Well, he felt downright ashamed that he couldn't even tell Bannister if Travis Quinn was alive or dead!

Hell, it was embarrassing! And it galled his hide having it all happen with these three dumb hardcases looking on. *That* was what really burned him up.

* * *

Daddow had worked himself into a state by mid-morning and the only tracks they had found might have been a week old. Shack picked up a pony's track but it was unshod and there were few wild Indians in these ranges who had firearms.

It wasn't Bird, anyway, for both his horses were shod.

Bannister would be tearing his hair by now, Daddow told himself. Hell, it had been almost a week and he *still* couldn't tell the man if Quinn was dead or alive for sure. If only that goddamn Bird hadn't quit and run out like that!

Then Cam made the breakthrough late in the afternoon.

He let out a wild war-whoop — the pre-arranged signal — and the other three came riding in fast, guns drawn. Cam pointed up the slope and Daddow frowned.

'What!' he snapped impatiently. 'All I can see is a dead wolf!'

'Yeah — he's drug himself to where he died. He's been gut-shot, Marv! A bullet's all tore him up . . . You see where the blood-trail comes from?'

Now Daddow saw what the hardcase meant — the trail of dried blood and torn entrails came down the slope from what he had figured was just a shadow cast by an overhang of rock. But he could see the edge of a small cave up there now . . . He turned to the others.

'Spread out and we'll go up on foot. Have your guns ready. You see anythin' move, stop it — dead.'

They hesitated.

He had made them jumpy now: the thought that Quinn could be lying in that cave still alive — and had somehow acquired a fire-arm — didn't make them eager to rush the small cave . . .

But at a sudden, savage, cursing order from Daddow, they charged up-slope, shouting, crowding in, diving for the floor, Shack firing his rifle before he could stop himself. He earned a whole bunch of obscenities as the flattened bullet slammed and snarled around the confined space, finally spending itself in a muddy wall near the tiny spring.

There was no Quinn. But there was a crude bed of boughs, a fireplace, strips of bloody rags.

And three more dead wolves. one impaled on a broken spear.

'He's bad hurt by the looks of all that blood and pus on them rags,' Crow reported to Daddow. 'But he's had help to get outta here.'

He pointed to tracks in the damp soil between the bed and the spring. Daddow struck a match and looked at the tracks carefully, just the toe of a worn riding boot.

'Son of a bitch's got the luck of the devil with him! . . . Well.' He stood slowly, keeping his head bent so he wouldn't hit it on the rocky cave roof. 'Let's go take it away from him!'

* * *

Quinn's rescuer was Firebird.

He had followed Quinn's trail to the cave, even though Daddow and the others hadn't been able to find any sign. And he had arrived just in time to save Quinn from the wolves.

The man had passed out and for a time the old Indian thought he was dead. But he went out into the early light, brought up the horses and, showing surprising strength for a man his age with such thin arms, he boosted the fever-ridden Quinn onto the pack horse, roping him in place. He mounted the Appaloosa and led the way into the trees.

It was slow going, having to dismount every few yards and go back and work over the tracks. He even took time to lay a couple of false trails and then he led the way into a stream and followed it way back into the hills until it began to narrow as it neared its source.

He kept climbing, slowly, laboriously, and on a ledge when he paused to catch his breath and wipe the sweat from his eyes, he looked down and way, way back, he saw movement. Those keen old iron-grey eyes picked out the four men spread out through the timber. Just seeing the colour of their mounts was enough for him to identify Daddow and his hardcases.

Well, from what he'd seen of their tracking abilities, he wasn't worried they would find him way up here. He doubted if they would even be able to trail him as far as the mountain stream, let alone spot the place where he had left it.

By afternoon, just as Quinn started to come round, moaning for water, Bird brought them to a grassy bench fringed with thick brush and timber, and backed by an almost vertical granite rock-face. Daddow and his men had long since dropped out of sight. He untied Quinn and got him off the chestnut, gave him water from his canteen, then drank sparingly himself.

'You sleep some more,' Bird said to Quinn, who was only semi-conscious again. 'I come back with medicine and grub . . . '

It was all a blur to Quinn. He lived half in the real world and half in a nightmarish world of his own, inside his burning brain. He merely nodded and passed out once more . . .

When he came to, his left arm hurt like hell, feeling as if someone had seared him with a branding-iron. He tried to move it and couldn't. But his head felt clearer.

It was dark and the small fire he could see across from his blankets was no more than dull red embers.

Blankets! . . . Fire! What the hell . . . ?

Something stirred and he jerked back instinctively as a man's shadow rose from near his feet and crawled towards him.

'Who — ?' His throat was parched and the word came out in a harsh, scratching grunt.

A bony hand pushed him back on his blankets with surprising gentleness yet with a firm pressure that brooked no argument.

'Drink.'

He felt the cold metal of the canteen against his scaled lips, brought up his right hand and held it, spilling water down his chin and neck. That was when he found out his left arm was strapped to his chest with a mixture of rags and strips of animal hide.

'Firebird?' he grated. 'Hell, I must be still delirious!'

'Fever broke now. You be okay — I cut wound, drain it, seal with hot knife after I bleed you. Change poultice later. Now you sleep.'

'Hell, Bird, I feel like I been sleeping for a week!'

'No. Just t'ree, mebbe four day.'

Quinn was quiet for a time as the Indian crouched by the fire, stirred it into life, and pushed a coffee pot into the flames he had revived.

'The wolves — that was you doing the shooting?'

Bird grunted without looking round. 'Talk later.'

'I'd like some of that java,' Quinn said. 'And I'm hungry.'

Bird turned slowly. 'White man! Always the red man's burden!'

Quinn surprised himself by grinning: he hadn't thought he had a grin left in him. 'Same old griper . . . No wonder Captain Marks was glad to be rid of you.'

Bird grunted again, looked over his shoulder and said slyly, 'He get rid of you first!'

'Hell, I just never re-enlisted.'

'Good days, the cavalry . . . You save my scalp, Quinn.'

'Hell, Bird, that must've been nigh on seven years ago! You ain't beholden to me still!'

'Mebbe not now,' the Indian said and Quinn nodded gently.

He knew what the Indian meant: he had saved Quinn from the wolves, treated his wound, brought him here — wherever 'here' was — and that surely was enough to square away any debt Bird figured he owed him from the cavalry days.

'Bird — you know there's some men after me?'

'Uh . . . Daddow hire me to track you down — twenty dollar and *Ozark Chew* tobacco . . . I find your track and leave.' He spat a short brown stream into the edge of the fire.

Quinn arched his eyebrows and

before he meant to, asked, 'You broke your word?' He knew that was unheard-of for an Indian of Firebird's status and the old Indian smiled and handed Quinn a mug of coffee.

'No break word — he hire me to track you down. I track you. It only fair I keep payment. Don't have to tell about you.'

Quinn actually laughed at that. 'You ain't changed any, Bird!'

* * *

They spent five days on the grassy bench, protected from the winds and the rain that had been beating down for more than twenty hours by the high granite cliff.

Bird had scouted around, reported that he had seen Daddow's bunch twice. They were lost themselves, he figured, riding in circles, snapping at each other, worrying more about finding their own way out than locating Quinn's tracks.

Whatever small trail sign may have remained would now have been washed away by the rain.

Quinn's arm progressed well now that it had been drained of poison. His body responded, too, to the better food Bird collected. Wild turkey roasted over the flames; a deer that gave them venison to eat now, and dried strips of meat to take with them when they moved on. Bird also used wild herbs. Then he made him exercise the arm, massaged the damaged muscles, brought him rocks of varying weight to lift.

'Hell, Bird, I'm gonna have a left arm twice as thick as my right, I keep this up!' complained Quinn.

'You have left arm that works,' Bird told him shortly, and made him do ten more push-ups using the damaged arm.

'I'd feel a lot better if I had a six-gun or rifle,' Quinn said, panting, streaming with sweat. 'I figured to make a bow, but a gun is what I really need.'

'Only have rifle. We move soon, stay

ahead of Daddow. You not need gun.'

The old Indian was wrong there, as it turned out . . .

The rain eased off as suddenly as it began and within two hours the sun was out, the ground steaming, and the sky a glowing blue, dotted just here and there with back-lit puffs of white cloud.

'Good time to go,' Bird said. 'Mud close over tracks. Leave till later and it be dry enough to hold sign.'

Quinn didn't argue. With returning strength came a restlessness and he wanted to move, do things, even if he didn't know where he wanted to move to, or what things he should do . . . 'Bird,' he said, sitting astride the sway-backed chestnut as the animals waded across the swollen stream, both horses deciding it was time to defecate. 'My head's kinda funny.'

The Indian looked at him but refrained from commenting. His expression said everything he thought about *that*.

'No, damnit! Not just because I'm a

white man,' Quinn added hurriedly, knowing how Bird thought of the white race. 'I was shot in a stagecoach hold-up — they left me for dead and when I came to, I couldn't remember the last few years of my life . . . All I knew was my name was Travis Quinn.'

'You got other name.'

Quinn frowned. 'How'd you know?'

'Manimato — Bear-Who-Walks. Your Lakota name.'

Quinn half-smiled. 'No, didn't mean that, Bird . . . I had another white-man name, Dave Callahan. There's a — woman. And a child — I don't remember them. Only that I am Travis Quinn and something happened to me up this way in the San Luis Valley . . . Memories are coming back: I recall Daddow, Sheldon Bannister and so on . . . But I still feel — lost.'

Bird had been watching him closely and now they heaved their mounts up the stream bank and the Indian indicated which way to turn.

'You right. Head all messed up . . . You in big trouble you have Bannister for enemy.'

Quinn nodded. 'I know — I ain't got it quite sorted out yet, but I know he forced me to ride the outlaw trail.'

'Uh? You ride with Kidder?'

'Yeah! That's what I need to sort out — Stew Kidder! I'm not sure where he fits in, except I know I rode with his bunch for a spell . . . '

'Kidder hide out here, in Wolfpacks.'

'Yeah, old feller named Gadsen told me that much . . . You know where I can find him?'

Bird shook his head and sometime later said, 'Mebbe find out.'

Quinn didn't bother asking how. Bird would do it if anyone could.

Wearily, he followed the old Indian, exercising his bad arm as he rode, still wishing he had a gun to call his own.

* * *

They had been lost for a time, but somehow, by good luck or plain accident, they had found their way back to the tumbling stream. None of them would admit how relieved they were.

The four manhunters looked hollow-eyed and gaunt as they watered their trail-battered mounts.

'How long we gonna keep it up, Marv?' Crow asked huskily, voicing what the others wanted to ask but weren't quite game. 'Speakin' for myself, I've had a bellyful.'

Shack and Cam moved uncomfortably under Daddow's gaze and turned back to seeing about their horses.

Daddow scowled. 'Fact is, I'm fed-up, too, and — '

'Marv!' Shack called abruptly. 'Come lookit here! Comin' from upstream! Fresh hoss-dung!'

'Judas!' Cam exclaimed. 'It could be them, Marv!'

Daddow took one look, coming to life again, shaking his head abruptly.

'Mount up an' let's go find out!' He fought his thirsty mount back from the water's edge, danced a little as he tried to get his boot in the stirrup. 'And if it *is* them, this time we really finish it! Leave 'em for dead and get the hell outta these lousy hills! The wolf packs can clean up after us!'

The others grinned in anticipation at finally ending this long chase and climbed aboard their mounts, spurring away upstream.

Daddow was a bit apprehensive: Bannister didn't want Quinn dead right now. He had a use for him. But — the hell with it all!

Daddow was a man used to regular shaving if not bathing, enjoyed his tailor-made clothing, and generally appearing neat and tidy — setting him apart from the usual rag-tag cowpoke.

All this time in the wilds, unwashed, clothes worn and torn, the frustration of the search — well, like Crow, he'd had a bellyful.

But what he had to do was make sure one of the other three finished Quinn. Give Bannister someone to blame and keep himself in the man's good books.

8

Outlaw Country

The country was too rough on the horses. The animals were tough but too old for the prolonged climbing and zigzagging across the rugged face of the slopes that the men required of them. They had to dismount and lead the weary animals and when it came to clambering across these harsh slopes, Quinn realized just how much he was lacking in stamina.

His breathing came hard and short and his head swam. His arm and shoulder were sore but his legs were weaker than he figured.

He was forced to sit on a weathered deadfall in order to settle his breathing and slow his pounding heart.

Bird glanced back, face unreadable

as usual, kept going until he reached the next ledge.

'I wait five minutes,' he called down.

'Go to — hell, Bird!' Quinn gasped. 'Take me — a — a goddamn half-hour — to get — up there.'

'I be gone then — you wasting breath, white man.'

Quinn cursed him, glaring coldly. 'I'm only half-white, damn you!'

Bird grunted. 'Use other half then. That the good half.' He spat an arcing stream of tobacco juice, looking off into the distance, apparently indifferent to Quinn's distress.

Quinn couldn't help but smile — a little. 'Lousy Comanche!'

'Weak-leg Lakota,' Bird said without heat. 'Why they call you Bear-Who-Walks when you don't?'

Quinn didn't answer, heaved to his feet, and started up the slope again, dragging the old chestnut at reins' end.

Bird began to move on before he was halfway to the ledge, but he got there in just over ten minutes.

And had to take another rest.

There was a bend in the trail that hid Bird from him when he started out once more and he was surprised to find the old Indian waiting on a rock, cheeks bulging with a chew of Ozark . . . as if he were saving the juice . . .

Quinn stopped, frowning. 'Legs give out, Comanche?'

Bird sent an arcing stream of brown juice so accurately that Quinn had to move aside so quickly he stumbled. There was maybe the suggestion of a smile on the Indian's face. He pointed down-slope by a lifting motion of his jaw.

Quinn turned his head to look and stiffened.

Riders! Moving through the trees down there!

'Daddow?'

Bird nodded. 'Spreading out. Must've found tracks.'

Quinn watched the four men, each with a rifle balanced on his thigh or held out to the side in one hand, moving their horses through the rocks and timber. The animals covered the distance up the slope three times faster than Quinn and Bird.

'Well, now's the time I could use a gun,' Quinn said and started when Bird handed him his battered old rifle.

It was a Henry that had seen much use and it had a lot of worn, sloppy parts. The trigger went almost all the way to let-off before there was even the slightest pressure. The tubular tin magazine showed where the dents had been repeatedly banged out over the years.

'Bullets feed all right?' he asked Bird sceptically.

'Bang butt — that free 'em.'

'Christ, with a trigger as sloppy as this you'd be lucky not to blow your head off!'

Bird reached up, took his head in both hands and made as if he was trying to twist it off. He shrugged his shoulders and Quinn sighed.

'What're you gonna do?'

'Give the mountain to them,' Bird said enigmatically nodding towards the men below and started away across the slope. Someone spotted him and a gun crashed twice. Quinn saw the lead strike several yards down-slope.

He got the horses behind the nearest rocks and climbed down into a space between two jammed deadfalls and some man-sized boulders.

Daddow's men were calling excitedly to one another now, urging their horses on faster. There were three more shots but the bullets were short and wild.

Quinn couldn't use his left hand properly to hold the rifle's fore-end. It still hurt too much. So he rested the barrel against a boulder on his left, used body pressure to steady it and his right hand to lever a cartridge into the breech. Someone below let out a whoop and came charging up the slope, mighty eager. Quinn beaded him quickly and triggered.

Bark exploded from a tree to the rider's left and the man hauled rein fast, lifting his face to see where the shot had come from. It was Cam, and struggling with the awkward levering, Quinn got off a second shot as the man spurred across the slope into thicker trees.

The bullet whined away, and as he fought the lever once more he watched the others converging now, ready to charge up-slope. Bird had disappeared but Quinn knew he didn't have to worry about the old Indian.

They raked his shelter with concentrated fire, and he crouched, grimacing as rock chips and splinters from the old deadfalls whipped around him. He fired at Shack, saw the man's horse plough its nose into the slope and send the rider spinning. Shack skidded and rolled as he slid away in a wild fall, losing his rifle.

More lead hammered into Quinn's meagre shelter and he heaved back, moving more deeply beneath the rocks.

When he looked back, he saw that Cam had dismounted and was running up, dodging from tree to tree.

Quinn levered, got the gun up fast. Cam's weapon lifted, rested against a tree trunk for steadiness. They fired together, and Quinn's shot tore bark and sap from the tree, Cam rearing back, clawing at his eyes. Quinn didn't know where Cam's shot went but he managed to work the lever while holding the rifle with his bad hand. The excruciating pain it caused, luckily, did not affect his aim.

Cam jerked in mid-stride and went down against the slope, fingers clawing at the gravel. Quinn fired again and the man jerked once more, flopped onto his face and was still . . .

Daddow came charging in, urging his horse on with spurs and curses, rifle raised to his shoulder. Quinn fumbled the reload and the gunman got off a shot that ruffled Quinn's hair. He threw himself over the rock he had been leaning against. Two more bullets ricocheted off his new shelter and he heard the clatter of hoofs as Daddow raced by.

Quinn rose to one knee, shooting, the lead taking Daddow's hat off, sending it spinning to the slope. The man spun, almost unseating himself, and the horse panicked as it started to lose balance. It leapt wildly, regained its footing but was already sliding down-slope.

Crow and Shack hurriedly got out of the way, triggering wildly at Quinn. Then Crow looked up and hauled rein instantly.

'Christ! Look out!' he yelled, wheeling his horse and running it recklessly down the slope after Daddow's panicked mount.

Shack glanced up, and took off on foot as if the devil himself was chasing him.

At the same time, Quinn became aware of a muted rumble — and then felt the first tremors through his prone body as the mountain shook.

Next instant there was an avalanche of rocks and stone and deadfalls spinning end-for-end, spilling over the slope before him. Dust choked him, fistsized rocks bounced against his shelter, shaking it. Then a rain of smaller stones pattered across his back and head. Sticks struck him in the face, and large boulders bounced and thundered, smashing down young trees, flattening bushes, sweeping the slope in an unstoppable flood . . .

The thunder rumbled on and on and on. The boulders kept coming, pushing splintered trees before them, ploughing the slope to destruction . . .

Suddenly, there was only a pattering rain of smaller stones and swirling, choking dust. He coughed as he waited for it to clear.

The landslide had swept down the mountain to the left of where Cam lay and piled up in a massive heap at the base. Quinn looked for the others but they were nowhere in sight. Just as well they weren't trying to charge up the mangled slope again, because Quinn was exhausted and his chest heaved as he spat and fought for breath.

Bird had literally 'given the mountain

to them' by starting that avalanche — however he'd done it . . .

He was reloading the Henry when a gun-belt and six-gun thudded at his feet, followed by a scarred and dusty Winchester rifle. Quinn looked up swiftly as Bird clambered down over some rocks, his back to Quinn.

'Find the guns under the big boulder you levered up to start that landslide?' Quinn asked as he examined the holster rig and the rifle.

'Cam,' Bird said, found his footing and turned slowly, holding out something else in his hand. 'This, too.'

Quinn jumped when he saw what the object was.

A still-dripping scalp.

* * *

Cam supplied them with one other thing: his horse. The animal, no doubt seeking company after the fright of almost being swept away by Bird's landslide, walked up to them as they were preparing to start over the crest. Its saddle was partly askew and splashed with some of Cam's blood.

It was a muscular buckskin and carried the B-Five brand. It nuzzled Quinn's bad shoulder and sent him staggering, just as he was trying on Daddow's hat with the bullet hole in the crown. It was a tolerable fit and he turned, grinning.

'Hey! Easy, you jughead!' He patted the animal, twigged its ears lightly, stroked the muzzle. 'You've had a scare, huh, boy? Well, just you relax, feller. I'll look after you from now on.'

He watched Bird adjust the saddle on the buckskin while he held its head and asked quietly, 'Why'd you take Cam's scalp, Bird?'

'Keeping hand in — might be other Indian war one day.'

'Come on! What'd he do to you?'

Bird looked at Quinn over the horse's back. 'He smart-talkin' man.'

'He bad-mouth you?'

Bird shrugged. 'Bad-mouth no one, now.'

Quinn knew that was all he would get out of the Indian and Bird helped him aboard the buckskin.

It was time to push on.

* * *

At the foot of the mountain, Daddow and his men took stock of themselves. Shack lay crushed by the avalanche, buried somewhere beneath tons of rubble.

Crow had been hit by a bouncing rock and had a bloody kerchief tied about his head, not showing a lot of interest in anything much.

Daddow had escaped virtually unscathed, just a few gravel scars here and there, nothing serious. He limped across to the stream and washed up. Crow sat holding his head between his hands. Daddow, standing in his sodden clothes, stared at the jumble of shattered rocks and trees on the slope. He swore bitterly.

'Take us a couple days to get round that mess,' he said half aloud. 'They'll be long gone by then. An' you can bet that Injun won't leave no tracks for us to find.'

'I need a sawbones,' Crow said abruptly. 'I can't see proper and I been throwin' up — could have brain damage — like that bronc buster we had on the Five a few years back.'

'Well, you ought to be safe,' growled Daddow. 'I ain't seen any signs that you've got a brain.'

Crow scowled. 'I'm poorly, Marv! And the hell with you, anyway.' He lurched to his feet, swaying, blinking as if to clear his vision. 'I'm goin' back . . . '

Daddow's jaw bulged as he clamped his teeth together, his cold eyes narrowed, watching Crow struggle to get a boot into his stirrup. He made no move to help.

Crow settled awkwardly in the saddle and said, 'We ain't gonna catch that bastard Quinn — not as long as that old Injun's helpin' him, Marv.'

Daddow continued to glare sullenly, looking murderous. Then he spat. 'Yeah, the hell with it! We need to outfit ourselves properly . . . Least we can tell Bannister — beg pardon, *Mister* Bannister — that Quinn's still alive.'

Crow cleared his throat. 'Wish you wouldn't keep sayin' 'we', Marv . . . I got no hankerin' to be there when you report to — Mister Bannister.'

Daddow smiled crookedly, mounting, curling a lip as he settled into leather in his sodden clothing. 'You'll be there — both of us will! Now, let's head back to the Five . . . But my bet is we'll be back here in a couple of days. Mr B ain't about to let Quinn slip through his fingers again.'

Crow groaned and set his mount slowly after Daddow's.

* * *

Claire's heart hammered up into her throat and a small cry escaped before she could stop it. Donny, playing with a baby shingle-back lizard, looked up quickly, saw her face. He jumped to his feet.

'Daddy come?'

She clasped the boy to her. 'I — don't know, darling. But — well, there is dust in the high pass . . .'

They were both scheduled for disappointment.

Sheriff Bud Hardiman rode in with another man, a big, thick-wristed fellow with a hard face and drooping frontier moustache. He wore a dusty, battered, high-crowned Stetson hat, and frank blue eyes stared out of the shade cast by its wide brim. He looked hot in his worn frock-coat and buttoned vest. He wore a single six-gun, high on his left side, butt to the right.

Hardiman introduced him as US Marshal Kent Hausmann, and the newcomer touched a large, gnarled hand to his hat. 'Finally caught up with them stagecoach robbers . . . ' began Bud Hardiman, but broke off as Hausmann swivelled his blue eyes towards him. He cleared his throat, made an 'over-to-you' gesture with one hand, ears reddening a little at the hard look the Federal man threw him.

Hausmann turned back to Claire, his face softening a little. 'Need to talk to you about your husband, ma'am — Dave Callahan, I believe, is the name he goes by?'

She tilted her head stubbornly. 'That's his name, yes — what d'you want to know?'

'Quite a lot, Mrs Callahan — wonder if we might move into the shade of the porch? And after you've heard me out, I'd sure like to look through your husband's room and belongings . . . '

Claire stiffened, heart hammering wildly again. 'I — I don't see why . . . '

Hausmann almost smiled. 'It's my way, ma'am. You see I've been lookin' for your husband for three years now and well, I can explain better out of this sun.'

She hesitated, nodded, then turned and started back towards the ranch house. Hausmann put out a hand as Hardiman started his horse forward.

'You can get on back to your stagecoach bandits, Sheriff . . . I'll be takin' over this Quinn case from now on. Thanks.'

'Listen, this is my bailiwick . . . ' bristled Hardiman, but once again broke off under Hausmann's hard stare. 'Aaaah! You Federal Johnnies are all the same! Glory hunters!'

He swung his horse around and spurred away towards the ridge. Hausmann watched him go, faintly amused.

* * *

Quinn, wearing one of Cam's shirts from the saddle-bags and Daddow's hat, swivelled in the saddle, looking around him, trying to figure out just where they were. But he had never been this deep into the Wolfpacks — not that he could recall, leastways.

Bird was leading but gave nothing away and Quinn was too damn tired to talk. This was really rough country, mostly rocks underfoot and hard on the horses. The buckskin was the least bothered by it, being younger and stronger than Bird's old horses, but even he protested at some of the places they went.

They had hidden out for a week after the gunfight and Quinn's arm was almost back to normal now. Then, one morning he found the Indian was missing. Knowing Bird's ways he spent the day tuning his fire-arms. He was satisfied with their performance now although the rifle pulled to the right some. But he didn't do much shooting, half-afraid the sound might bring unwanted visitors, be they wild Indians or men on the dodge checking there wasn't a posse entering their domain. Maybe even Daddow.

Bird didn't arrive back until after dark, suddenly appearing out of the night as silent as a wraith. He went straight to the small fire and helped himself to coffee.

'Not many beans left,' Quinn said, trying to act casual although he was eager to know where the old Indian had been.

'Stew Kidder might give us some.'

Quinn paused as he poked more wood on the fire. He merely looked at Bird. The Indian ate some jerky and beans, looking everywhere but in Quinn's direction. Quinn sighed.

'All right — I'll ask: where you been?'

'See tracks of Indian yesterday. He been watchin' us. So I wait for him and we talk. He take me to camp. Small tribe, only one gun among them, no young squaws . . .'

'Bird!'

'Okay— they know where Kidder is. They tell me, but I had to give them the Appaloosa. They very hungry.'

'Judas! You been walkin' in this country?'

Bird ignored such a silly question: how else could he have gotten back to the camp?

'Bird, I appreciate your sacrifice.'

'Left the Henry with 'em, too.' He moved and picked up something that, in the darkness, Quinn had thought was his rifle when he had first arrived. But it was a bow and a deerskin quiver of arrows. 'Bow and arrow good. Like old days. It fair swap for Henry.'

Quinn looked at the old Indian with affection.

'Bird, I'll buy you new guns and a decent horse when we get out of this.'

'You think good, Quinn — save me asking.'

'Can we get to Kidder's hole-in-the-wall?'

Bird looked at him sharply. 'Why call it that?'

Quinn frowned. 'I dunno — name just came into my head. Why?'

'Well, that where he is — in a hole-in-the-wall, west of — '

'Nightjar Rocks!' Quinn broke in. 'Yeah, I recollect now! The rocks seem to end against an unscalable cliff, at the end of a narrow canyon or pass, but — there's some kinda entrance . . . hidden by bushes. Lots of bushes . . . '

Bird arched his eyebrows: it was unusual for him to show surprise. 'You been there before?'

'Yeah — when we were on the run after a stage hold-up. It was the first time Kidder trusted me enough to take me to his main hideout . . . ' Quinn looked around him at the darkness, alive with the rustlings and calls of the night animals. 'Dunno as I can find it again, though . . . '

'Find tomorrow.' Bird's old eyes studied Quinn. 'You start to remember good. Soon know everything. Maybe even where wife is . . . '

And now here they were working their way through the waterless, heat-hammered canyons of the Nightjars, a rugged spur of the Wolfpacks themselves.

The heat dried them out like old leather left in the sun but neither man touched his canteen. This was country where a man conserved not only his water, but his food and energy as well — it had deterred many a posse in the past and would again in the future.

It was starting to come back to him by the afternoon, when they reached the narrow trail that climbed up and over a rocky ridge with a small, tight pass penetrating it and known, according to Kidder, as Sabre Cut.

Quinn recalled that he had spent many an hour atop the pass on lookout: all of the gang took turns at it, for a single man with a good rifle could hold off a large posse from up there.

'Bird!' he warned. 'There'll be a guard!'

He no sooner spoke the words than a rifle crashed and a bullet kicked gravel a yard in front of Bird's old chestnut. The animal whinnied but was too weary and old to rear up and paw the air in protest. As Quinn slid the Winchester from the saddle scabbard, the guard fired again. The bullet passed close to Quinn's head and he jerked aside.

'Call out!' the man above shouted.

'Travis Quinn! And that has to be you, Deadeye, shootin' that close!'

There was a long drawn-out silence as the echoes of the gunshots faded.

'Quinn's dead,' the man called down finally.

'I'm no ghost, Deadeye! This is Bird, friend of mine — we want to see Stew!'

'Who's behind you? You bring a damn posse in here?'

'Hey! This is *Quinn*! You ever know me to lead a posse to our hideout?'

'Not this one,' the man said and Quinn chilled.

What the hell did that mean . . . ?

'Deadeye — let's just see Stew, OK?'

'Yeah — I reckon he'll *want* to see

you, Quinn! But he ain't got no use for Injuns!'

The rifle crashed hard on the guard's last word and Bird grunted, somersaulted over the rump of the chestnut and landed sprawling on his back, arms outflung, shirt-front growing red with spreading blood.

9

Old Enemies

Quinn stumbled as he was hurled roughly against the side of the nearest cabin and he turned, the savage anger darkening his face as he glared at the outlaw called Stew Kidder.

'*This* son of a bitch wouldn't even let me go to Bird!' he snarled and threw off the hands that reached for him, knocking two outlaws to one side as he stepped forward and drove a boot against Deadeye's shins.

The man hadn't been expecting an attack there and he howled, stumbled, danced about as Quinn, moving like lightning, snatched the rifle from him and smashed the butt into his gaping mouth.

Deadeye went down hard, spitting teeth and blood, sobbing, moaning as he rolled on his back, hands half covering his face.

Before Quinn could do any more damage, the outlaws closed on him and Stew Kidder kicked his legs from under him. He fell sprawling and they were kneeling on him, slugging with fists and knees, cursing him bitterly.

Dazed, bleeding, Quinn was yanked upright and flung back against the cabin wall again. This time the two men holding him — Dallas on the right, Lewis on the left — leaned their weight on him and kept him pinned. Deadeye was barely conscious, almost choking on his own blood. Stew Kidder used a boot toe to heave him onto his side, where the man gagged and retched.

Kidder was large, starting with a pumpkin-like head, a negligible neck, shoulders like a brush bull, and a torso like a grizzly. He was beard-shagged like the others but it was wilder, hairier, and Quinn knew that it served to help disguise a mangled lip . . . *He* had been the one who had mangled that lip — with a red-hot branding iron. Not here, though, in another canyon where they'd been working on a herd of Bannister's cows . . .

Then the rest of it came to him: he had flung the running iron at the others, and as they scattered he lunged for his mount, vaulted into the saddle and charged through the yelling, staggering outlaws. He drew his six-gun and triggered two shots. One man — he thought he remembered his name had been Ray someone — staggered, clutching at a bloody chest, and the others had scattered for their mounts.

A hellish chase! Two days through some of the roughest country even in the Wolfpacks. They had trapped him on a narrow cliff trail that dwindled to almost nothing — and a hungry cougar had barred his path. He shot the animal but only wounded it, and it had leapt with a shrill scream at Quinn. He was dismounted and dropped to one knee, the horse's reins wrapped about his wrist.

The cougar had landed on the horse and, both animals screaming, locked together, had gone over the side.

And dragged Quinn with them. His head struck the trail's edge . . . He lifted a hand now and touched the deep star-shaped scar above his left temple.

That had been the wound that had taken his memory . . .

Now he glared at Kidder as the man ran a hand through his long, straw-coloured hair, pulled his lips tight across big teeth.

'Well, never figured to see you this side of hell, Trav . . . When you went off that cliff, drug down by your hoss *and* that damn cougar!' He shook his head slowly. 'You got more lives than a cat.'

'I'm usin' 'em up too fast for my liking,' Quinn told him, struggling against Dallas and Lewis. He watched Deadeye slowly coming out of it, sitting up groggily, holding a cupped hand under his shattered mouth as the blood flowed. The man lifted his cold, yellow eyes to Quinn's face.

'He's mine, Stew!' he grated, the words all slurred because of his injuries. 'I shoulda put a bullet through him when I nailed that old Injun.'

'And that's somethin' you're gonna regret, you bastard!' Quinn told him, a promise in his words.

Dallas cuffed him across the mouth. 'Shut down, you double-crossin' son of a bitch! . . . We're all gonna stand in line for a crack at you, Quinn!'

Quinn shook his head, tasting blood where his teeth had cut into the inside of his cheek. 'I dunno why you blamed me for that posse showin' up in the canyon where we were changing the brands on those cows, Stew.'

Stew Kidder came a step closer, bending slightly from the waist to look bleakly into Quinn's face.

'Because you was the only one that'd been outta the goddamn canyon in a week! Few hours after you got back, a posse showed, local law from Catamount. Lucky we had that herd of cows to stampede at 'em and give us a chance to get away . . . '

He hit Quinn a short, brutal blow in the midriff and the man gagged, legs buckling, held upright by Dallas and Lewis. He fought for breath, lights whirling and bursting behind his eyes, battling to stay conscious.

'Damn it, Stew! I only went to — get Rachel away safely — Bannister was closing in on her, and — '

Kidder reached out a big hand, cupped it under Quinn's jaw and wrenched his head up. 'Yeah — little Rachel! Reckoned she knew all about Bannister and then — disappeared. Mebbe she sent the posse.'

'Hell, no,' Quinn said. 'She was so scared she nearly wet herself just telling me Bannister had somehow gotten a line on her — I got her out best I could and come back to you and the gang.'

Kidder studied his face. 'Mmmmm — mebbe. You coulda been recognized when you put her on the stage an' a posse followed you. But I never figured you for bein' that stupid . . . Anyway, mebbe Bannister got to Rachel, 'cause she ain't been seen since you sent her — wherever you sent her.'

Quinn nodded slowly. 'Well, I ain't any too sure about that . . . But I don't think Bannister's forgotten about her. His men like to've half-killed me back in the lower Wolfpacks, but he sent Daddow after me. Maybe to finish the job, but I've got a hunch it was to take me back and make me tell where I hid Rachel.'

'Now *I'll* make you tell *me*! If she really knows somethin' that'll nail Bannister, then I can put that same info to a lot better use than she can. Or you!'

Then Travis Quinn laughed — and they all stared at him: Kidder, Deadeye, Dallas, Lewis, the shadowy forms of other gang members and a couple of women who lived in the camp — they must have figured he was crazy.

'You're outta luck, Stew — I don't recollect just where I sent her! Bird, that old Injun that Deadeye was so damn quick to put a bullet in, was the one who knew, and I've only just figured out he was trying to help me remember in my own time. But he'd've taken me to her eventually.'

Deadeye growled, and as he started to get to his feet, Kidder reached out a long, tree-like leg and pushed him roughly, sending him sprawling.

'You stupid bastard!'

Deadeye glowered. 'How the hell was I to know? Christ, you think I can read minds? You sent me to watch the Sabre Cut and that's what I done, Stew! Don't go takin' your craw out on me!'

For a moment Quinn thought he had succeeded in causing a rift between Kidder and his crackshot. It looked like Kidder was going to draw his Colt and shoot Deadeye on the spot, but then he smiled crookedly and turned back to Quinn. The smile faded to a grin entirely without humour.

'Still up to your old tricks, huh? Don't matter, Trav. I got you now and you're gonna tell me anythin' I want to know over the next few days. I've lived with lousy Injuns, too, know their ways.' Suddenly he spat, his face hardening. 'Lived? Hardly the word! They made a goddamn *slave* outta me for a coupla years before I got away — but I learnt a few things while I was there, just keepin' my eyes open. Like how to keep a man right on the edge of dyin' for days, a week . . . You know what I mean, bein' part-Injun.' He lashed out and hit Quinn again, this time in the ribs. 'Mebbe that's why I hate your guts!'

He hit him twice more, then jerked his head at Dallas and Lewis. 'Take him out and nail him to the door of the barn through his hands. Let him hang overnight and see if he feels more like talkin' come mornin'.'

Lewis, a dark, good-looking man with slicked-down hair, smiled and said, 'He'll sure feel like somethin' by then! Like *hell* is my guess!'

That raised a laugh and Deadeye, on

his feet now, lurched across to Kidder. 'Stew — lemme do it! Lemme nail him up, okay?'

Kidder shrugged. 'Don't take too long — I want you back up on the Cut before dark.'

They started to drag Quinn towards the old weathered tarn and he bucked and fought but Deadeye hit him in the kidneys and his boot toes dug twin trails in the dust as they got him as far as the door, spread him out like a cross. Deadeye ran into the barn, humming now despite the pain in his mouth, and came back with a hammer and handful of long, rusty nails.

'Git his hand opened out!' he slurred impatiently, yellow eyes bright now.

They fought Quinn but his shoulder let him down and his left arm was soon stretched out across the planks, fingers bent back by Dallas . . . Deadeye grinned with his ghastly, bloody mouth, pushed the blunt point of the thick nail against Quinn's palm and swung the hammer up for the first blow.

Quinn tensed himself for the excruciating pain to come . . .

'Don't worry, Quinn,' breathed Deadeye. 'I'll go slow and easy — make it last!'

The hammer swung down and there was a strange thunking sound and Deadeye seemed to push in against Quinn's body as the front of his chest bulged for an instant before a flint-tipped arrow burst through his flesh and blood spurted as he fell screaming, nail and hammer dropping to the ground . . .

The others froze — and Quinn reacted with a speed and efficiency that had to be inherent, acquired over many years until it had become an instinct, a lightning-swift action.

As Deadeye fell, clawing at the arrow that had impaled him, blood pouring from his mouth, Quinn wrenched free of the startled outlaws, snatched at Deadeye's six-gun. His hand closed over the butt and the man's continuing fall extracted it from the holster.

'Watch him!' bawled Stew Kidder, more alert than the others, pulling Dallas across his body as Quinn dropped to one knee, the Colt blazing. Dallas shuddered, his body driving back into Kidder and taking the man down in a tangled heap.

Quinn twisted and triggered again. Lewis, starting his draw now, reared back against the barn door and screamed as another arrow pinned him through the shoulder. The rest of the outlaws, who had come to witness Quinn's crucifixion, were only now starting to react. Quinn brought down one man in midstride, shot another's leg from under him. One of the women screamed and ran and one of the men still on his feet snatched her blouse, ripping it as he pulled her across in front of him. He snarled as he swung up his gun and Quinn took a quick bead on him over the screaming, struggling girl's shoulder and fired. The outlaw's head snapped back and he went over, dragging the girl down with him.

Two more men decided they had had enough and started to run into the deepening shadows cast by the high rock walls of the hidden basin as the sun dropped rapidly. One fired two token shots without even looking but the other concentrated on saving his own hide.

Quinn didn't know if all six shots had been used or not as he swung back towards Kidder who had extricated himself from beneath Dallas' bleeding body, looking wildly dishevelled as he thrust to one knee, his own Colt rising at arm's length.

Quinn dropped hammer — and it fell on an empty chamber. Kidder grinned tightly, but before he fired a third arrow took him low down in the side, almost in the hip, and he grunted, spun swiftly, dropping the gun as he clawed at the dangling shaft. It had not gone in deeply, just enough to hurt.

Quinn leapt up, ran in and kicked the man savagely in the head. Kidder sprawled, unconscious. Quinn snatched up the man's fallen gun but there was no one left to shoot at now. They were either dead or wounded, or had disappeared into the deep shadows of the walls.

Sweating, he stood, looking briefly at Lewis who was sobbing in pain, still trying to pull the arrow free of the wood. As he saw Quinn looking at him, he lifted his free hand, empty, shaking his head.

'I'm — out of it, Quinn! Just get me down!'

'Stay put,' Quinn told him and kicked guns out of reach of two wounded men. Dallas was dead, as was the man who had tried to shield himself behind the woman. Kidder was unconscious, Quinn stood amongst the bodies, gunsmoke wreathing his lower legs. He looked at Deadeye, then took a quick line from the position of the man's body to a clump of rocks halfway between the barn and the hidden entrance in the wall.

'Bird?'

A grunt, and then he was sprinting forward, looking about him alertly in case some of the others found their courage and made another try for him.

He found the old Indian sprawled in his own blood amongst the rocks. His bow, his last arrow nocked in the string, was held in his left hand. Even in the dim light, Quinn saw the greyness of the weathered skin, the sunken look to the high cheeks. But the iron-grey eyes met his steadily enough as he knelt and lifted the bloody shirt-front. He fought to keep his face blank as he saw the wound: there was little hope for Bird. Maybe if they could get to a doctor within an hour or two he might stand a chance but . . . out here . . . Bird was as good as dead.

'I see Great Spirit — soon,' Bird gasped.

'Hell, Bird, you done almighty good!'

Quinn started to tear up the old man's shirt-tails and pressed the cloth over the wound, and the Indian grunted, stiffened. 'Sorry, *amigo*.' Quinn eased up on the pressure. 'Bird — there ain't a lot I can do, old friend . . . '

'Great Spirit wait — I go easy now — I kill my — enemy.'

He rolled his eyes towards the sprawled men outside the barn and Quinn knew he meant he had killed Deadeye, the man who had shot him: it would mean easier passage into the Spiritland for him . . .

Quinn shook his head slowly as he thought about what it had cost Bird to drag himself all this way, the life pumping out of him with every movement . . .

He jumped when Bird began to chant — it was his Death Song but the words were barely intelligible and he kept gasping for breath. Quinn held the old, gnarled hand in his but there was no return pressure. The iron-grey eyes began to slowly glaze and the chant died away. He made two or three more attempts to complete it but without success.

The dulling eyes turned to Quinn's face.

'Not — Cheyenne — ' he gasped, rolling his head. 'Cheyenne — you — 'member . . . You — me — get — '

The word drifted into guttural gibberish, and in moments the old man was dead. Quinn folded his arms across the bloody chest and picked up the bow. It was reinforced at the tips with deerhorn, adding strength. He wondered how on earth someone as old as Bird, and with his chest blown open by a .44 rifle slug, had had the strength to not only loose off one arrow with enough force to transfix Deadeye, but to fire twice more, once pinning Lewis to the barn door . . .

He stood, briefly arranging the braids as he laid the bow and the remaining arrow across the stilled chest.

Then he walked back to the barn

door where Lewis had almost passed out. He gripped the hickory arrow shaft, snapped it off and wrenched Lewis free. The man shouted in pain and collapsed at Quinn's feet, barely conscious. Stew Kidder moaned and began to move, one hand rubbing at his throbbing head, eyes not yet in focus. Quinn looked at two more wounded outlaws.

'You fellers want to light-out, now's your chance. Stick around and I'll likely finish the job on you before I leave.'

The men, nursing their wounds, nodded, and staggered away towards the corrals. The remaining woman ran out of the nearest cabin and joined them, saddling a horse for herself.

Quinn shook Kidder. The man moaned, focused, and glared. 'There was no need for this — I only wanted to know if you recollected where I took Rachel. Seems you don't.'

Stew Kidder scowled. 'I been lookin' for three goddamn years! How the hell you figure *I* might know where she is?'

Quinn shrugged, rubbing the scar on his temple. 'Memory's not back in full yet — I didn't recollect we'd had such a falling-out — but you're wrong about me bringing in the posse. I dunno whose doing that was, but it wasn't me.'

Kidder glared. 'Mebbe I b'lieve you — coulda been Rachel herself . . . I dunno. Well, you've about wiped me out,' he added, gesturing to the two wounded men and the woman riding out towards the hidden entrance. 'What you gonna do now? Finish me off?'

'You'd be no loss to the world, Stew, but I guess not. 'Less you try somethin' stupid, then I'll shoot to kill.'

'You're as fast as you ever was,' Kidder allowed grudgingly. 'That was somethin' I always liked about you, Trav . . . You had some good moves, and a lot of quick. We coulda cleaned up big, working from here . . . '

'You blew the chance, Stew.'

'All right, all right — in this game you never know who to trust. You get suspicious about someone and you better do somethin' pronto or you'll be lookin' at the world with a rope knot under your left ear.'

Quinn was studying him as if making up his mind about something. 'The old Indian kept saying 'Cheyenne' before he died . . . Why would he do that?'

'Hell, he was your Injun — but if it was somethin' to do with Rachel you can forget it — I been to Cheyenne and looked for her. She weren't there.'

Quinn frowned, feeling the goose-bumps on his flesh. Damn! He had been almost sure that was where he had sent Rachel — Cheyenne, Wyoming . . . It was the first thing that came into his head after he'd come to down in Arrow Creek, New Mexico: his wife Rachel, in Cheyenne. But three *years* ago!

Bird had been trying to tell him something when he died. 'Not Cheyenne . . . Cheyenne . . . ' and the rest of whatever he'd tried to say. The hell did it mean? Or did it mean *anything*? The old Indian was dying, dreaming his spirit was rising out of his body on its way to meet the Great Spirit — his mind must have been wandering . . . 'Not Cheyenne . . . '

Hell, Stew Kidder claimed he had searched for Rachel in Cheyenne without result. And Stew Kidder would have looked thoroughly. So Bird *must've* meant something else . . .

Hell almighty: now where did this leave *him*?

In an outlaw hideout with wounded and dead men for company . . . no confirmation at all about where he thought he had left the woman he had known as Rachel . . .

For a moment, his mind went back to the other woman who claimed to be his wife — Claire Callahan. And the tousle-haired boy, Donny. *His* child, she told him . . . But the only 'wife' he could remember was Rachel . . .

'When did I marry her?' he asked suddenly. 'Rachel, I mean?'

'Hell, don't ask me. I dunno if you was married or not. An' din' care then, don't care now. You *said* you was married and she'd come on down from Cheyenne. After you come back that last time, you said you'd sent her back to where she come from, which I figured meant Cheyenne. But if you can recollect where you really stashed her, we can make ourselves a small fortune — or do you already know what she's got on Bannister?'

Quinn half-smiled. 'Blackmail, Stew? A little outta your line, isn't it? And dangerous with a man like Bannister.'

Kidder shrugged. 'You figure livin' the way I have these past ten years ain't dangerous, dodgin' lead and Injun arrows? Hell, I got two arrowheads in my hide, been winged half-a-dozen times by lawmen or bounty hunters — a little blackmail don't faze me none. Not even goin' up agin someone as mean an' miserable as Bannister.'

'We gave him a pretty rough time, huh? You and me?'

'Hell, he kicked you off your place

and you ran into me and my bunch liftin' some B-Five cows, pitched right in and helped out, and when the Five nighthawks got organized and came after us, you fired Bannister's pastures so as to keep 'em busy while we drove off the cows.' Kidder shook his head and there was admiration in it and in his crooked smile. 'Knew I couldn't afford to lose a man with talent like that.'

'So I joined up with you.'

'Yeah — Bannister had an interest in a stage line at that time and we give him many a headache holdin' up his coaches. He'd kicked out most of the sod-busters along the river bottoms and we got a few recruits. Lewis was one, Tatum another . . . Oh, Bannister don't like you and me, Trav. Not — at — all . . . I reckon we kinda stopped his ambitions dead . . . '

'Then the cougar put me off that cliff and when I came to I thought I was someone else, ended up in New Mexico.'

Kidder arched his eyebrows and his tone was sceptical. 'That so? Now you're back to square up with Bannister? Or . . . me? Or . . . what?'

'What, I think — might have to take care of Bannister along the way, but mostly I want to get my full memory back. It's comin' — slow but sure — I see places and suddenly I remember 'em, and what happened there. Sometimes that leads to other memories, sometimes only to a dead end — '

While he had been talking, Kidder had held a wadded bandanna against the arrow wound in his side. The head had sliced a gash in the flesh but had fallen out without deep penetration. There was a lot of blood, though.

'What you gonna do now?'

Quinn glanced at the semi-conscious Lewis and then towards the dark shape of Bird. 'Give Bird a proper burial so he's facing the right way so he can meet the Giver of Life . . . '

'Christ, you actually b'lieve that Injun stuff?'

Quinn didn't bother answering. 'Then . . . I guess I'll just keep on goin'. Bannister's sure to have someone on my trail still. And I reckon I took Rachel somewhere north of here, so . . . '

'Want company?' Quinn arched his eyebrows at the question and Kidder shrugged. 'Well, you ain't left me much here. Up to you to make things up to me, huh? What d'you say, Trav, old pard? We was a good team once, can be again. You an' me agin the world — an' to hell with 'em all!'

Yeah, Stew Kidder was a good man to have along in case of trouble. Only thing was, you couldn't trust him worth spit.

10

Twisted Trails

Daddow wasn't happy about any of this.

Here they were, back in the Wolfpacks, with a full expedition, pack-mules loaded with enough stores to keep them in the wilderness for a month. That was one thing he *really* didn't like: the idea of staying out here *that* long.

Another was that he only had two men to back him: Crow, who was okay in any kind of a scrape, and a man called Utah who had been riding for B-Five for only a couple of months. But in that time he had beat up some sod-busters, burned down a barn and a cabin, and generally raised hell with the stubborn families along the river bottoms who were hanging on to their quarter-section parcels of land tooth and nail. He was a mean type, wall-eyed, and with teeth too big for his mouth so that when he spoke a man had to stand well back to avoid being sprayed by spittle.

Daddow could admit to himself — and no one else! — that he was jealous of Utah, for the man had a mean streak a mile wide and a willingness for violence, if not killing, that matched his own. He was afraid that Utah might even replace *him* one day . . .

But the *real* thing that galled him on this trip was that Sheldon Bannister himself had decided to tag along.

'Only way I can be goddamn certain sure of getting the job done!' the rancher had snarled when Daddow and Crow had reported back. 'Christ, four of you go in there and only two come out, both licking your wounds! And after chasing just *one* man who was supposedly half-dead by your own admission!' Bannister had heaved out of his chair and stalked around his desk, lips moving in muttered curses. He had stopped dead suddenly, and raked both Daddow and Crow with a savage gaze. 'Tell me — just what the hell do I pay you for? No — tell me what you do to *earn* the money I pay you!'

Daddow knew better than to give any kind of an answer, but Crow was stupid enough to shuffle his feet and try to justify his existence as a B-Five hardcase earning fighting wages.

Bannister jumped down his throat with both boots as Daddow had known he would — and he felt some satisfaction about him doing it, too — and Crow had subsided, looking as if he wished he were somewhere else . . .

Anyway, it ended as Daddow had feared it would: Bannister had tagged along and the man was making things harder than ever, bitching about this, that and the other thing every second minute. Complaints, complaints, complaints . . . until Daddow just caught himself as he was about to ask

Bannister why the hell he didn't just turn around and go back and leave the manhunt to them . . .

He knew how wide open he would be leaving himself if he was loco enough to ask a question like *that!*

Now here they were, deep in the Wolfpacks on the third day, caught amongst tortuous canyons with high walls that made the trail they were using stifling and airless. Heat hammered down, affecting men and beasts.

'How much longer in these damned canyons?' demanded Bannister, but Daddow pretended he didn't hear, swinging his attention to Utah who had ridden on ahead to scout.

The man had appeared suddenly on a small rise and was waving his hat in the agreed signal: two full sweeps left-to-right. That meant he had spotted someone.

Jesus! Let it be Quinn! Daddow prayed silently, urging his weary mount forward to meet Utah. 'Well?' he snapped.

'Couple fellers and a woman,' Utah told him, spittle glinting briefly in the sunlight. 'They look as if they been shot — the men, leastways. Woman seems all right, but she's jumpy as a frog on a stove-top. Keeps ridin' on ahead, swingin' back, yellin' at the others to hurry up.'

'Where?'

Utah pointed, half-standing in the stirrups. 'Over yonder rise. We wait in that draw, we'll be able to jump 'em as they come up here — if you've a mind to, that is.'

Daddow glared. 'I'll tell you what I've a mind to — and whatever it is, you just do it, savvy?'

Utah had a long, well-used face, and he nodded, smiling faintly. 'Whatever you say — boss.'

'Don't take that tone with me! You — aaaah! Yeah, all right, we wait in the draw and jump 'em . . .'

'What is it?' snapped Bannister riding up on his long-stepping sorrel, sweat beading his flushed face.

Daddow told him and the rancher was glad to get into the shade of the draw. They waited twenty minutes before the trio Utah had spoken of appeared. Two men — both with gunshot wounds — and a woman who looked to be unscathed but mighty nervous. She screamed when the men rode out, covering them with guns.

One of the men swore, wheeled his mount and tried to make a run for it. Utah brought him down with a single shot between the shoulders. Bannister snapped his head around, glaring. Utah looked innocent.

'We still got the other one and the woman,' he said casually. 'I don't mind workin' on her for a spell.'

Bannister scowled, turned to the wounded man who had his hands in the air now.

'Hell, that's Tatum!' exclaimed Crow suddenly. 'One of the sod-busters we run off couple year back, Mister Bannister!'

The rancher put his sorrel close to

the man, staring into the dirty, beard-shagged face, seeing the bloody bandages around his lower chest. They were bright with fresh blood. Without taking his eyes off the man's face, Bannister slammed his rifle barrel across the wound.

Tatum howled in pain, lurched, starting to topple from the saddle. Bannister helped him all the way out and when he sprawled on the ground, walked the sorrel forward to straddle the gasping man. He leaned from saddle and poked him in the neck with his rifle barrel.

'Who shot you, Tatum?'

Tatum bared his teeth. 'Go — to — hell!'

Bannister didn't like that, levered a shell into the rifle but before he could shoot the breathless, wild-eyed woman said, 'A devil named Quinn done it, Mister!' she gasped, her words bringing Bannister's head around quickly. 'He come into Stew Kidder's hideout like a runaway train, killed or shot-up half the gang, includin' Stew himself . . . We was lucky. He kicked us out . . . Look, Mister, all I wanna do is get down to Catamount. I can find a job there . . . I got no argument with anybody . . . '

Bannister's eyes narrowed. 'You can take us to this hideout?'

She nodded quickly. 'But I guess Quinn ain't there now. He didn't seem as if he was gonna stick around.'

'You just take us there and you'll have nothing to worry about, my dear.' Bannister turned back to Tatum. 'Seems I don't need you any more, sodbuster.' And he shot the man through the chest. The woman screamed and Bannister snarled. 'Shut her up! And let's get moving!'

Utah hit the woman and set his mount alongside hers as she sobbed, and led the way back over the rise.

Bannister rode alongside Daddow. 'See what I mean about doing the job myself? I've already got more results than you did in a couple of weeks!'

Daddow said nothing but his teeth

made a grinding sound . . .

The only living being they found in the hidden basin was Lewis. His wounds had been bandaged and he told Bannister readily enough it had been Quinn who had done it.

'He took off with Stew.'

'Where were they going?' Bannister asked mildly.

Lewis shook his head. 'Somewheres north — Quinn's gone lookin' for that woman he called his wife — Rachel.'

'Is he now? That's what I want to hear — and Kidder?'

Lewis slid his gaze away. 'I — dunno. He's wounded, but he — wants Rachel, too, I reckon. He never did like her.'

Bannister held his gaze to the man's face, turned to Crow. 'See if you can get anything more out of him . . . Marv, burn these cabins and the barn . . . '

'What about me?' the woman asked. 'Can I go now?'

Utah's face was tight with anxiety as he watched Bannister and the rancher smiled crookedly at him.

'You want to . . . escort the lady out of here, Utah?'

'Sure, Mister Bannister! Be glad to.'

The woman tried to spur away but Utah laughed, grabbed one arm and dragged her out of her saddle and across his lap where she kicked and thrashed. Laughing and whooping, he rode into the nearest patch of brush.

Bannister saw Daddow's face as the man gathered deadwood and stacked it against the cabin! 'You don't approve?'

'No — but I guess that makes no nevermind.' He struck a match.

Bannister nodded. 'Glad to see you still know your place . . . All right, hurry up and let's get out of here.' He looked around as the first flames licked at the cabin. 'No wonder we could never find that son of a bitch Kidder . . . but we'll get 'em both this time. Quinn won't be expecting us so soon. And this time he'll tell me where that bitch is hiding!'

Daddow didn't quite agree with that: he had worked up quite a bit of respect for Travis Quinn these past couple of weeks.

* * *

'Not Cheyenne — Cheyenne . . .'

The words drifted down through the murk of Quinn's dreams and set him to rolling about in his bed-roll.

His dreams these nights were badly mixed-up: he had trouble sorting them out, failed to understand most of them, and none of them seemed to bring back any incident that would trigger his total memory recall.

He *felt* he was almost there — something just beyond his reach kept tugging at him, trying to tell him something. And that 'something', he felt, was the trigger he needed to regain all of his memory.

But this dream tonight — it had been about his boyhood with the Lakota Sioux, and had somehow drifted into his association with Bird. A tangled run of sequences from their cavalry days together — barely remembered now — and finally he saw Bird standing on a flat rock with one edge broken away so that in silhouette it resembled a turkey's head. The old Indian's arms were spread and he leaned forward, shouting, '*Not Cheyenne . . . Cheyenne . . .*'

Wells! The name smashed into Quinn's brain and his eyes flew wide and he started half-upright on his bed-roll. 'By God! It was Cheyenne *Wells* where I took her — no. Where *Bird* took her! I handed her over to him and he . . .'

His heart was hammering now and he hardly noticed that it was almost daylight. But he saw Kidder stir and prop himself up on one elbow, squinting sleepily.

'You say somethin'?' the outlaw slurred.

'Dreaming,' Quinn told him curtly. 'Time to get up anyway.'

'The hell for? We been wanderin' around in here for a couple days and you got no more idea where you're goin' now than when we left the Hole.'

Quinn, jamming on his hat first in the timeless tradition of cowboys, then starting to pull on his boots, smiled crookedly. 'Mebbe I do now.'

Kidder scowled. 'You ain't so much Injun you're gonna tell me you *dreamt* it!'

'You know a flat mesa with one side broke-up so that it looks like a turkey's head from some angles?'

Kidder came alert. 'Turkey Mesa — man, that's way the hell east of here in . . . Injun country.'

Quinn smiled. 'Let's eat and ride . . . '

Kidder didn't pursue it, but he watched Quinn sidelong all through the preparations for breakfast and, afterwards, the saddling of the horses.

He checked his weapons before they moved out of the campsite.

Kidder led the way through the tangle of the Eastern Wolfpacks and down out of the hills, onto flat country that stretched for some miles before broken crags once again reared against the blue Colorado sky.

The outlaw was tense as they started out onto the flats. It made him jumpy being out in the open like this . . . He was a man who was used to living no more than a few yards from some kind of cover, where he could dash and set himself up to shoot it out if danger threatened. Here — well, anyone back on the last ridge of the Wolfpacks would be able to just sit comfortably in the shade of a rock or tree and watch their progress until they made it across these open flats and into the gnarled terrain on the other side . . .

* * *

Standing with one boot atop an egg-shaped rock beside the small spring trickling down from above, Daddow lowered his glasses and turned to where Bannister and the others were resting, smoking.

'You fellers feel like stirrin' yourselves, I've got 'em — they're headin' into that wild country with all the crags and buttes and mesas . . . We can't overhaul 'em before dark. But at least we know where they are . . . '

Bannister was beside him, snatching the field glasses, and impatiently asking, '*Where*? *Where*, for Chrissakes?' Daddow pointed, easing Bannister's shoulders in the right direction. 'Right, I see 'em — Marv, just what the hell is out that way, beyond the mesas and stuff?'

'Injun country. Wild Horse Mountain tradin' post at Kit Carson's old camp on Sandy Creek . . . Nothin' then till the Kansas line.'

'Yeah there is,' said Crow. 'You got that Injun reservation at Cheyenne Wells . . . '

Daddow didn't like admitting to a mistake and he jerked his head curtly. 'Wasn't countin' that,' he growled.

'Well, you damn well better count it!' Bannister snapped. 'We count *everything* where Quinn's concerned . . . The man's a half-breed. There could be some connection between the reservation and him . . . We'll stay here till dark then make the crossing.'

'Boss! — I mean, Mister Bannister!' Utah said urgently, pointing down to the flats. 'Another rider — seems to be followin' Quinn an' Kidder.'

Bannister got the glasses up to his eyes quickly, fumbled with the focus, mouth tightening. 'He's following 'em, all right . . . Dismounting, checking for tracks . . . Man in a vest and white shirt . . . See if you know him, Marv . . . '

None of the others knew him. After a while Bannister said, 'Makes no never-mind. We move out after dark. We'll follow 'em all!'

11

Pay the Price

They were heading for the distant flat mesa with the broken side, known as Turkey Top Mesa.

There were woods and crumbling rock on the approaches, and as they rounded one huge boulder the trail narrowed to pass between it and its twin, just wide enough for two horses abreast.

There was a rider sitting slap-bang in the middle of that narrow trail, big hands at the ends of thick wrists folded on the saddle horn. He wore a high-crowned Stetson, a loose-hanging vest over a once-white shirt, and there was a folded coat tied to the cantle. His sixgun was rigged high on his left hip for a crossdraw and frank blue eyes stared out of a rugged face, which was made older-looking by a bushy frontier moustache streaked with grey and nicotine.

'Howdy, gents.'

Quinn and Kidder reined down sharply and the big rider smiled thinly, still looking at Quinn. 'Remember me, Trav?' His left hand went to one edge of his vest and pulled it open enough for them to see the US Marshal's badge pinned to the shirt pocket. 'Come on! You know me — Kent Hausmann . . . '

'By Christ! I know that *badge!*' shouted Stew Kidder, and he lifted his rifle, thumbing back the hammer.

'Wait up!' Hausmann snapped, but Kidder wasn't waiting and after that Quinn wasn't too sure exactly what happened.

Kidder's rifle reached his shoulder but it was Hausmann's Colt that roared, two fast shots almost rolling into one another and, as Kidder flung up his arms and started to roll out of the saddle, a third slapped into him in mid-air, turning his body so that he landed face down in the dust.

He made no move — except one leg twitched three or four times.

By then, the smoking gun was covering Quinn who had belatedly started to reach for his own Colt — it had all happened that fast.

'Relax, Trav — he needed killin'. You're OK. You're one of us.' Hausmann squinted. 'You remember *that*, don't you?'

Quinn froze, then let his hand drift away from his gun butt, resting it on his thigh. The other was gripping the reins around the saddle horn as he frowned at Hausmann.

'Looks like it's true, huh? About you not havin' your memory back yet?' the marshal asked.

Quinn sighed. 'It's — coming. Slow but sure . . . '

'That's the way . . . You don't remember me, though?'

'There's — something stirring way back in my head . . . Something about — law — marshals . . . '

Hausmann looked pleased. 'I'll jog it along. You're a Deputy United States Marshal, Trav — all that outlaw stuff was Bannister's doin' and it just happened to fit in with your chore . . . See, you pin your badge to your underwear, while I pin mine to my shirt pocket — where everyone can see.'

Quinn frowned. 'Are you saying — I was — '

'Working undercover,' Hausmann finished for him, nodding. He slid the gun back into its holster, waiting patiently as Quinn struggled with swirling memories — and faces from the past . . . 'Looks like you need a mite more help, Trav.'

'Guess I do . . . There's someone named — Web? Webster . . . ? I can't quite pull it together.'

'Webber — Chief Marshal back at HQ. Yeah, he was the one sent you down here to check on Bannister. Got a parcel of land in your name so you'd be one of Bannister's neighbours and, to make it a leetle more authentic, he arranged a wife for you. You remember *her!*'

'Rachel?'

'That's the name she used but her real name's Serena.'

'We actually got married? I'm not clear about a lot of this . . . I sort of remember the Marshals now, but most everything else is still a kind of blur.' But he felt excited as the memories began to stir. Now that he was on the right track it shouldn't be long before he remembered everything. '*Did* I marry her?'

Hausmann shook his head. 'We gave her a wedding ring to wear and all you had to do was say you were married and act like it.'

'Who was she? Far as I recollect there were no women in the Marshals' service.'

'She came to us and said she'd been through Alamosa not long before and saw a man who called himself Bannister — but she was certain it was the same man she'd seen a year earlier down on the Border, runnin' guns and generally mixed-up in politics with the rebels in Mexico. His name was Mansell then — and he was responsible for killing the feller she was shacked-up with, a Mex government official named Miguel Estrada. Which is likely why she came to us in the first place. Her chance to get even.'

'You believed her?'

'Well, we've got a Ringo Mansell on our books as a wanted *contrabandista* and political assassin . . . This was too good a chance to pass-up and she was willing to go down and take another look at this Bannister and identify him for sure — as long as she had protection. Which was where you came in . . .'

It was stirring in Quinn now. The dark-haired, golden-skinned woman with the flashing eyes and the dazzling smile . . . All he had been told was to protect her, and to that end she was to pose as his wife. By then Bannister had put out the

Wanted dodgers on him for rustling and they had to hole-up with Kidder's and Stroud's bunch. The woman came to him not long after, said that Stroud, always a ladies' man, had been pestering her and she wanted Quinn to do something about it.

'Don't want to fall foul of Stroud *or* Kidder at this stage, Rachel,' he'd told her. 'I need them to keep the pressure up on Bannister so he's likely to make a mistake where we can come down on him hard and throw the book at him. This has to be done legal or he'll slip through our fingers. Once we've got him on this land-grab deal, then we can hit him with whatever you've got.'

He had not, at this stage, been told the details of Rachel's involvement: only that they needed her positive identification of Bannister.

'Then you get me out of here! Now!' she said, sounding frantic. 'I won't stay around Stroud.'

Her white teeth tugged at her full

lower lip and she added, 'I — it's more than Stroud. I'm scared of Bannister. I wish I hadn't come here — get me out of here and I'll go to Webber and keep my part of the bargain. But I can't stay here!'

She'd told him her story when he slipped away from Kidder, took her down to Catamount and bought her a stage ticket to Cheyenne. But Bannister and Daddow had been in town, and she was so scared he'd ridden out to Smoke's trading post to see Bird, asked him to help the woman, hide her out for a while. Then, when he figured it was safe, see she got to the Marshals' office. Bird, feeling beholden to Quinn because Quinn had saved his neck in the cavalry years before, had agreed . . .

'So that's how come she never showed on that stage,' mused Hausmann. 'Where'd this damn Injun take her? We looked for a helluva long time, never found any trace of her.'

'I left it up to Bird. I had to get back to Kidder.'

'Then why didn't he tell you where he hid her?'

'Never saw him again for three years . . . Then when I did I guess he figured to let me get as much of my memory back as naturally as I could. He was a wise old warrior and he did try to tell me where she was when he was dying but never quite made it.'

Hausmann looked at him sharply. 'So you teamed up with Kidder again — and Cheyenne Wells ain't too far away . . . Your Injun have kin at the reservation there?'

Quinn shrugged. 'I — think mebbe so. I never had much time to think about it. A posse followed me back to where we were using a running iron on some of Bannister's cattle and Kidder blamed me. I fell over a cliff during the chase, hit my head, and lost my memory. For the past three years I've been Dave Callahan down in New Mexico . . . '

'Arrow Creek,' cut in the marshal. 'Yeah, I know. Tracked you down after we heard rumours that Travis Quinn had come back from the dead, had a word with Claire, and she let me go through some of your things. I found an old map of this country, some parts marked in pencil, which I guess were Kidder's hideouts, so I came lookin'.'

Quinn felt tight in the chest. 'I don't yet recall that part of my life in New Mexico.'

'Well, guess you had that map on you when you lost your memory, maybe kept it around hoping some day it'd help you get back your real identity . . .'

'I can't recall, but mebbe you're right . . .'

'You figure this Rachel's still at the reservation?'

'Hell, no! But I'm hoping someone may tell me where she went . . . She was running scared of Bannister — '

Hausmann looked disappointed. 'Why do you want to find her now?'

'Thought it might help me get all of my memory back. Up until now, I thought she was my real wife and she was in Cheyenne. I thought Kidder might know where I took her, because I hadn't remembered about the Catamount stage at that time. Or that he blamed me for the posse finding his hideout.'

'Ye-ah — well let's go see for ourselves.' When Quinn hesitated, he added, quietly, but with authority, 'I'm still your field officer, Trav. Far as we're concerned, you're still a deputy marshal, so that still makes me your boss.'

Quinn shrugged and they rode around the mesa, looking for the wilderness trail that would bring them to the west side of the reservation known as Cheyenne Wells.

They hadn't yet cleared the mesa's shadow when there was a clatter of hoofs to their right and a bunch of riders thundered out of a cleft in the rock at the foot of the mesa.

Four men, white men, scattering now.

And with guns blazing.

'Bannister!' yelled Quinn as the lead whined overhead. They must have heard the shooting when Hausmann had gunned-down Kidder, he figured.

He slid his rifle free of its sheath and Hausmann unshipped his own Winchester, veering away from Quinn, making two wide targets. But Bannister and his men were ready for such a move. Two riders thundered hard after Hausmann, and the other two came after Quinn: Daddow and Crow.

He crouched low over the horse's neck, leaning down like an Indian and shooting the rifle one-handed under the mount's head. It jerked away and he almost lost balance. His shot burned the hide of Crow's mount and the man fought to get it under control. Daddow was standing in the stirrups, rifle to shoulder. Quinn knew the man would get a fairly good bead this way and when he saw a patch of sand to his left, threw himself bodily out of leather. The horse ran on as he ploughed into the sand, rolled and skidded. Bullets ricocheted from rocks above him.

He kicked his way into shelter as Daddow, sided once again by Crow now, came racing in, raking the patch of sand. Clouds of grit obscured Quinn's vision at first but he dropped to a prone position, working lever and trigger. Crow lurched, and dropped his weapon, clawing at his shoulder. He used his knees to veer his mount away, but it was too violent a manoeuvre and the horse stumbled, unseating Crow.

Quinn threw his aim to Daddow who was ready to swing in a tight arc and come racing back. He beaded the mount and fired. The horse broke stride, shuddered, and went down, forelegs folding beneath it. Daddow was thrown heavily, rolled dazedly about the ground as Quinn spun onto his back in time to see Crow running in. The man's left arm dangled limply from a shattered shoulder, and his teeth bared as he brought up his six-gun, firing again and again.

His bullets chipped the rocks and kicked up sand. But not for long. Quinn's rifle blasted as the man was only a couple of yards away and his body spun wildly, flopped over onto its side. Quinn swiftly put another shot into him, turned back to Daddow. Marv was savagely angry, his eyes bulging with the pressure of his wildness, clothes torn from his fall. He scrabbled around for his dropped gun and Quinn stood, firing from the hip. The bullet kicked gravel into Daddow's face and the man rolled away, cursing.

Quinn levered and triggered again: but the rifle was empty. He dropped it, reached for his Colt — only to find the gun gone — it must have fallen when he had dived out of the saddle. He ran forward as Daddow straightened, kicked the man in the chest, sending him sprawling again. Daddow was startled but he smiled crookedly as Quinn lunged in. A handful of gravel in Quinn's face stopped him dead and by then Daddow was on his feet, head down, charging like a bull.

Quinn was carried over onto his back and Daddow straddled him quickly, hammering at his face, locking his fingers around his throat. Blood roared in Quinn's head. His eyes stung. His tongue filled his mouth. He bucked and heaved, and, with a straining lurch, hooked one thumb into the side of Daddow's mouth. Daddow shook his head, felt his flesh tearing away from his jaw, released his stranglehold. Quinn flung him aside and they rolled away from each other, bouncing to their feet.

Then Daddow let out a wild yell as he spotted his pistol and scooped it up. Quinn dived for his legs and felt the blast from the Colt's barrel on his back. He locked his arms about Daddow's legs, thrusting with his shoulders, up-ending the man. Daddow clubbed at Quinn's head with the gun, but Quinn caught the hand in both of his, rammed a knee into Daddow's midriff, driving the breath from him.

At the same time, he twisted the gun

towards Daddow and the man's animal-like face was suddenly afraid as he looked right into the muzzle. It was the last thing he saw, except perhaps for the flash of flame as Quinn forced the man's finger against the trigger . . .

Quinn took hold of the six-gun as Daddow's hand went limp, heaved away and swung around to see how Hausmann was doing.

Utah was sprawled amongst some rocks, lying as if his back had been broken, face all bloody. Beyond, he saw Bannister, kneeling, pleading desperately with Hausmann who was still sitting his saddle, smoking rifle in hand. 'I only want to find the girl, Kent! Gimme a break!' Then Hausmann's rifle crashed, once, twice, three times, and when Quinn looked again, Bannister's broken body lay sprawled and bleeding on the ground. Quinn massaged his aching left shoulder, looked up at the marshal.

'Well, that's an end to it, I guess,' he panted, gesturing at Bannister's body.

'Don't have to keep on searching for Rachel now.'

Hausmann began thumbing fresh shells into his rifle, looking down at Quinn with cold eyes. 'We do.'

'How so? Seems pointless now that Bannister's dead.'

Hausmann shook his head. 'Bannister wasn't alone in that Border deal. We don't know if Rachel can put her finger on any of the others or not, so we still have to find her — and see. Bannister had inside help when he stole those rifles from Fort McKenzie. They never got a line on who it was. And there's a few pointers that make us think someone in high places is protectin' him. We aim to close the books on this one, Trav. It's been too long. This time we finish it.'

Quinn picked up his rifle and six-gun, glanced down at Bannister, his chest riddled with Hausmann's bullets. All three holes could be covered by a playing card. 'You don't take many prisoners.'

The marshal's face was sober. 'Just like you — you left more dead men along your back trail than you ever brought to trial.'

Quinn had nothing to say to that. He couldn't remember, but he did have flashes of gunfights, partial images of carefully laid ambushes . . . More and more memories were flooding in now. He could recall the assignment to get Bannister in a fair amount of detail. Sod-busters complained they were being run off their quarter sections by Bannister's men, then forced to sign over their deeds for a nominal sum so as to make it 'legal'. This way Bannister covered himself and the law was powerless to prosecute — Daddow and his men saw to that by beating up any sod-buster who stayed around Alamosa after being run off his land . . . In Quinn's case, Bannister forged the transfer and had Quinn declared an outlaw, forcing him to team up with Kidder's gang. Until Kidder blamed Quinn for bringing that local Catamount posse in . . .

But there was still a lot of confusion in his thoughts and memories. As they rode away from the dead men, he said, 'I guess Bannister must've realised I was looking for Rachel and he was using me to lead him to her . . . I dunno — seems to me Rachel ought to be left alone now. She risked her neck and managed to get out in time. Why hound her now?'

'Because I say so, damnit!' Hausmann growled. 'Hell, Trav, you used to be one of the toughest men we had in the service. This soft side is new to me!'

'Maybe to me, too, then — but it feels — comfortable enough.'

Hausmann moved in the saddle to glare at him steadily. 'Well, it all comes down to this, Trav: you're still a marshal — and you do like I say . . . And I say we look for Rachel. You got it?'

Quinn nodded slowly. He didn't like

it, but he would go along with the marshal — for now . . .

* * *

The Indian Agent, a man named Tuckett, told them, yes, Rachel was still on the reservation, he was pleased to say. The Indians called her *Amaya*, Beloved Woman.

'Came in three years ago with an old Comanche-Cheyenne and asked to stay for a couple of months — never left, she liked it here so much. Started a school for the kids, helps out in the infirmary — was a nurse in the war . . . We wouldn't know what to do without her now.'

'Where is she?' Quinn asked, and Tuckett pointed out of the dusty office window towards a small log building across the quadrangle.

'School's in today so that's where she'll be.'

Quinn started out right away but as Hausmann made to move after him the agent said, 'Hold up, marshal — I need you to sign my book, give your reasons for comin' onto the reservation — Indian Commission's mighty strict about it. You can sign for yourself and your friend . . . '

Hausmann glanced out the window, saw Quinn walking rapidly towards the schoolhouse, and then he nodded jerkily. 'Let's have it then . . . '

Quinn remembered her as soon as he saw her at the far end of the classroom, where she was writing on a blackboard, her back to the class of a dozen Indian children. They stared at him, wide-eyed, as he coughed, and she looked around, over her shoulder.

Her hair was braided like an Indian's and she wore a beaded headband. She gasped and dropped the chalk as she recognized Quinn.

'Travis!' she said in a whisper that carried easily to him down the room. She hurried towards him down the narrow aisle between the rows of desks, smiling tentatively. He moved to meet her, took her hands and they looked at each other and the memories came surging in . . . *good* memories.

The children were staring and she hesitated briefly, then kissed him lightly on the mouth.

'It's been so long, Travis! And I heard you were dead . . . This is so pleasant, you coming here!' She swept an arm about the classroom at the big-eyed, dusky faces. 'These are my children now . . . I'm so grateful to Bird for bringing me here. It changed my whole life. As soon as I saw these people, the indifferent way they were treated, their lives without direction, I realized my *own* life had been aimless, too. I knew I had to do something positive with my life, make myself more — useful. I'd indulged myself for too long — I'd once been a tutor to a New England family, so I started this.'

She waved at the children and Quinn smiled. 'You look happy, Rachel. I'm glad for you.'

Suddenly, she sobered, hands tightening on his. 'Travis — why are you here? Bannister?'

'He's dead, Rachel. But Marshal Hausmann still thinks you might have evidence about others that — what's wrong?'

She dropped her hands from his, put one hand to an amulet on a leather thong at her throat. 'Kent Hausmann?' Quinn nodded and she drew in a sharp breath. 'He's no marshal! He's a mercenary, works for the highest bidder. He even worked for Miguel once — he's the man who helped Bannister steal those guns from Fort McKenzie, the one Bannister hired to *kill* Miguel!'

She stopped speaking abruptly, looking past Quinn's shoulder, and he felt the slight draught as the door opened.

Hausmann smiled crookedly at the woman. 'Well, howdy-do, Serena — finally caught up with you. I should've killed you when I killed that snake Miguel — I don't like not finishing a job . . . But you've had it too good here for too long. Time to pay the price.' He faced Quinn. 'Orders, Trav, from high up. She's still a danger to certain people — Aw, no! You ain't gonna be stupid and try to protect her, are you?' He shook his head sadly. 'Man, I can out-draw you while I roll a smoke with one hand. Sorry I used you and took advantage of your memory lapse, but I ain't been paid to kill you, so unless you do somethin' really stupid . . . '

'Like you reminded me not long ago, Hausmann — *I'm* still a marshal!'

Quinn was very close to the edge of the door, and now he kicked it shut suddenly, viciously. Hausmann grunted as it smashed him out into the yard, and Quinn yanked the door open with his left hand, reaching for his Colt with his right, as he launched himself through in a head-long dive, taking the danger away from Rachel and the children.

He triggered while in mid-air as

Hausmann lurched to his knees, gun flashing into his hand and firing — but only once. Quinn's lead hammered the man down, rolling him onto his back, shirt-front and throat all bloody, smoking six-gun falling from his limp hand . . .

Quinn picked himself up, turned back to the doorway . . . He froze, sick to his stomach.

That single shot that Hausmann had managed to get off had found a target. Right between Rachel's breasts . . .

The Indian children were already starting to wail as he stood there, letting the returning memories swamp him . . .

* * *

Claire really thought her heart might stop this time.

She had had several starts, watching the high pass, seeing dust, hoping it was Dave returning. There had been only disappointment so far. But today she felt a strange tightness in her chest.

This time it really was him! She felt it, deep down . . .

'Donny!' she called wildly, looking around for the boy before she remembered he was in the barn, no doubt getting into some kind of mischief. 'Donny, come here! Quickly!'

Moments later the boy came running out of the barn as fast as his hard-pumping little legs could carry him up the slope to where she waited, trembling.

'Daddy? Daddy?' he called in a piping voice and she laughed as she swept him into her arms.

'Oh, darling, I hope so! *How* I hope so! It's been so *long!*'

And this time she wasn't disappointed.

The man she knew as Dave Callahan rode in a short time later, looking almost as weary as the traildusted horse. He dismounted stiffly and then his dark, sober face split into a smile and he held out his arms. Claire, still holding the boy, ran into them, laughing and crying at the same time.

He held his family tightly and said, 'It's coming back, Claire.' She knew he meant the memories of their life together.

'*You're* back, that's all that matters,' she told him.

He nodded, knowing there was no need for more words.

Travis Quinn, outlaw, late of the US Marshals' Service, had been left behind somewhere back there in the Wolfpacks.

Dave Callahan had come home.

THE END

Other titles in the Linford Western Library:

A TOWN CALLED TROUBLESOME

John Dyson

Matt Matthews had carved his ranch out of the wild Wyoming frontier. But he had his troubles. The big blow of '86 was catastrophic, with dead beeves littering the plains, and the oncoming winter presaged worse. On top of this, a gang of desperadoes had moved into the Snake River valley, killing, raping and rustling. All Matt can do is to take on the killers single-handed. But will he escape the hail of lead?

McKINNEY'S LAW

Mike Stotter

McKinney didn't count on coming across a dead body in the middle of Texas. He was about to become involved in an ever-deepening mystery. The renegade Comanche warrior, Black Eagle, was on the loose, creating havoc; he didn't appear in McKinney's plans at all, not until the Comanche forced himself into his life. The US Army gave McKinney some relief to his problems, but it also added to them, and with two old friends McKinney set about bringing justice through his own law.